By Max Allan Collins

THE X-FILES: I WANT TO BELIEVE
ROAD TO PURGATORY
ROAD TO PARADISE

As Patrick Culhane

BLACK HATS
RED SKY IN MORNING

THE (X)-FILES™

I WANT TO BELIEVE

MAX ALLAN COLLINS

Based on the screenplay by
Frank Spotnitz and Chris Carter

HARPER

ENTERTAINMENT

An Imprint of HarperCollinsPublishers

HARPER ● ENTERTAINMENT

An Imprint of HarperCollins*Publishers*
10 East 53rd Street
New York, New York 10022-5299

THE X-FILES: I WANT TO BELIEVE copyright © 2008 by Twentieth Century Fox
ISBN 978-0-06-168771-6

First HarperEntertainment paperback printing: August 2008

Printed in the United States of America

Visit HarperEntertainment on the World Wide Web at
www.harpercollins.com.

10 9 8 7 6 5 4 3 2 1

For my wife and son,
who spent so many Sunday evenings
with me, watching The X-Files

Scientists were rated as great heretics by the church, but they were truly religious men because of their faith in the orderliness of the universe.

Albert Einstein

THE Ⓧ-FILES™

I WANT TO BELIEVE

Chapter 1 _____

The day had been so overcast, Monica Bannan barely noticed dusk settling in, the last cold light of day doing its best to hold on to the somber colors of winter, and failing. Skeletal trees and occasional farm buildings were black shapes against a darkening sky, but Monica found them comforting, soothing, not forbidding, much less foreboding. Only when her car's headlights came on automatically did she realize that darkness was upon her.

The heater purred and she was almost too warm in the hooded sweatshirt, down vest, and sweats. Her curly blonde hair, however, combed back, damp (from her swim on the way home from work), would freeze out in that chill wind. But it would be only a few steps from her carport to her warm house. She could risk it.

With no makeup on, and her prominent nose, Monica looked almost plain, though she really was quite attractive—in her youth she had even done some fashion modeling. Now, approaching thirty, she was one of that army of professional women who worked for the government in nearby Washington, D.C.

She'd had a typically long, not particularly memorable day, and looked forward to a quiet evening in front of her TV with the fireplace going behind her and Ranger, her German shepherd-ish mutt, curled up beside her on the couch, big head in her lap.

The little housing development loomed ahead, dark boxy shapes in the descending night. The snow had stopped mid-afternoon but the roads were still slick enough, with patches of black ice, for her to take the turn into the settlement of small houses with extra caution.

Soon, however, without incident, she was pulling into the driveway and up into the carport beside her single-story clapboard house, its lights mostly off. Had her eyes been on her rearview mirror, she would have seen the bulky figure passing behind her, blushed red in her brake lights, ever so briefly.

But she did not.

She switched off the ignition, her medical ID bracelet swinging to strike the dashboard lightly, and she was about to go in—her things in the trunk could wait—when she heard Ranger going nuts in there.

By all rights she should have kept the animal outside—hadn't she gone to the trouble of putting in a doghouse in back? But with this cold, this awful goddamn arctic cold, how could she do such a thing to the only male in her life right now?

So Ranger was in there, yapping his head off, but it took a moment for her to realize that this was not a display of welcome-home affection, rather a vicious growl-tinged round of barking of a sort usually reserved only for cats and squirrels.

Monica opened her car door and stepped out, yelling, "Ranger! Be a good boy! Settle down in there! It's just *me* . . ."

But she had not even started toward the nearby house when she saw something that contradicted her: *footsteps in the snow.*

Monica froze in place, almost literally, her damp hair already stiffening despite the hood; she was still under the roof of the carport, if barely, her mind working to overcome the fear rushing through her bloodstream.

If Ranger was barking, these footprints were fresh . . .

She took a step back, Ranger's frantic muffled barking still in her ears, her eyes searching the back wall near where she stood, where an array of gardening tools nestled, waiting for better weather. Perhaps one of these could provide the weapon she needed to help her make that short, endless trip to the house; she had a gun in there, after all.

That was when the figure in heavy winter gear, thermal jacket bulging like steroid-enhanced muscles, appeared before her, breath pluming, the big man's face barely visible in the near darkness, though she somehow made out rugged angles and light-color eyes colder than the wind.

He saw her.

He moved toward her.

He reached for her.

She grabbed up the gardening tool with its soil-ripping attachment and, as if she were carving her way through dense jungle, drew it back and came down with it, swinging it, slashing.

His gloved hands came up, reflexively, but the sharp prongs caught a wrist, tearing flesh, and leaving red jagged trails across one cheek as well.

Ranger's barking seemed to pick up as Monica spent half a second marking her path to the house, but the next half second took that possibility away, as another intruder stepped out of the dark to block her.

This second big bulky figure in winter gear had long, dark, greasy hair and an angular, unforgiving face from which breath emerged like smoke.

Rasputin, she thought.

The gardening tool, with its long handle, was

too big and awkward to run with—a part of her brain chastised herself for not grabbing something smaller—and she could do nothing else except toss the thing toward the first intruder. The second one had his hands on her, grasping at her, but she was already running, taking off toward the woods way at the rear of the row of houses.

Once in the trees she could circle around and get help from a neighbor; but first she needed to get away from these hulking attackers, put some space between her and them . . .

She was in good shape, and she was slender and lithely muscular and she could make it. She could make it.

Only they were as fast as they were big, and she could hear their footsteps behind her, crunching snow and ice and the twigs and leaves beneath, and their heavy but not labored breathing made a disturbing percussive counterpoint to her own fear-tinged, quicker intakes of breath, cold steam streaming from her lips.

Words from the Frost poem tumbled in her brain in a refrain of quiet hysteria: *Woods are lovely dark and deep . . . miles to go . . . promises to keep . . .*

And they were on her.

She heard Ranger barking, barking, so very far away, but he could do no more than she could about these men who were blotting out what little light remained.

As they overcame the struggling young woman, her

two arms no match for their four, Monica Bannan had no idea that the medical ID bracelet on her wrist held a special significance to these men . . .

. . . just as these men did not know they were making a mistake in choosing this particular victim, whatever her qualifications might be.

Because these inhabitants of a night just arrived did not know they had selected, for their malign purposes, an FBI agent.

Rural Virginia
January 9

The FBI search team left their black SUVs along the roadside and headed inland. The white stuff was deep enough to have men and dogs thrashing at it, and sun reflecting off the unending white landscape meant most of these searchers chose to wear sunglasses. A wide line moved across the designated area, heading toward woods on the horizon, and every man and woman, including Assistant Special Agent in Charge Dakota Whitney, wore a black jacket with FBI in prominent yellow.

With one exception.

One man wore a gray jacket and gray slacks. Underdressed for this harsh weather, the tall man in gray, his hair a wild nest of gray and black, his pale oblong face touched with the gray of a goatee, pleasant features clenched with concern, tromped out ahead of the law enforcement team. The government searchers, including the dogs, were following this single civilian.

"*Give him room!*" Whitney told her colleagues, even though a part of her wondered why. She had to be mad to take such a desperate action. But her fellow agent Monica Bannan was missing. And action, desperate or not, needed to be taken. They had tried everything else, every recommended procedure plus a few that were not on the books.

But nothing they had tried was more off the books than this.

Tall, slender but formidable, her long dark hair tucked under the hood of her FBI parka, the blue-eyed beauty who was ASAC Dakota Whitney had not risen to her position by playing it safe. At thirty-six, she was known as smart and tough and willing to take risks and even cut procedural corners if a case called for it. And Whitney would do whatever it took to find her colleague, her friend . . .

Right now her eyes, and her hopes, were pinned on that unsteady human scarecrow trudging through the snow.

Wheeling unsteadily, almost as if intoxicated, his dark eyes filled with nervous intent, their civilian point man paused to call to the FBI searchers: "It's *here* . . ."

And he was on the move again.

So was the FBI.

The wind was howling now, a high-pitched quality to it, as if the sky were laughing at their efforts.

The sky had a point, Whitney knew, but she was not laughing, nor smiling, her gaze fixed upon the tall man's every step, steps at once certain and uncertain, as this wild man seemed to know exactly where he was going, if he didn't go down on his ass first.

Up ahead, he turned, as if on strings managed by an insistent puppeteer, and seemed about to fall, and perhaps make a snow angel; instead he broke into a run, slowed but not stopped by the drifts he traversed.

Whitney and her team swept hard after him, though as many eyes were on the ASAC as on the man they followed.

She called, "*Let him go*—let him go. Just stay with him."

And the wild-haired man in the gray jacket was running hard in the deep snow now, his breathing labored, his steps difficult but unceasing. This was a man with a mission, a man possessed . . .

And suddenly their unlikely leader fell on his hands and knees, as if he'd collapsed; but he hadn't. Like a miner who'd found gold, he cried out, "Here! Here!"

"Go!" Whitney cried. "*Go!*"

"Here! *Here!*"

In seconds the FBI agents, with Whitney at the fore, surrounded the wild-haired man, who might have been sunk in the snow, praying.

But he wasn't. Not right now, anyway.

He was digging, with his gloved hands, scooping

away white with ever-increasing urgency and speed.

Whitney leaned in, half disgusted with herself for taking this shit seriously, half hopeful that their unlikely guide might have actually led them somewhere.

To something.

And then the white gave way to a grayness that might have been dirty snow but wasn't: this gray had once been pink, and was of a texture quite unlike the white around it.

Whitney said, "*Stop!* I'll take it from here."

But her own gloved digging was hardly any more scientific than the wild-haired man's, and he was still digging, too. They had both seen the same thing, human flesh, grimly discolored, and the sick feeling in the pit of Whitney's stomach was soon replaced by relief, and then confusion.

Their guide had led them to something human, all right: *a severed arm.*

And, yes, Whitney was relieved that this was a man's arm, not a woman's, that this detached limb could not, *did* not, belong to Special Agent Monica Bannan.

But to Monica's disappearance had been added a second mystery: *What man had this arm belonged to?*

And why did it have a jagged cut along its wrist?

Chapter 2 _____

Our Lady of Sorrows Hospital
Richmond, Virginia
January 9

The doctors seated at the conference table had their attention on another medical professional, a cool-eyed, self-confident African-American woman in white. This distinguished-looking, authoritative figure sat not at the head of the table, but rather spoke to them from a flat-screen monitor on the wall.

"I've gone over the charts you sent," the doctor on the satellite feed told them, "and consulted another pediatric neurologist who works with me here. And I must say we're alarmed by two things."

Dr. Dana Scully said, "The deficiency in lipid metabolism and the severely diminished enzyme output."

All eyes, including those of the disembodied head on the video screen, went to the striking red-haired woman who'd spoken so matter-of-factly. With her long Titian tresses touching the shoulders of the white smock, Dana Scully had the lovely features of a Gibson Girl circa the start of the twentieth century; but here in the first decade of the twenty-first century, this petite, shapely woman of forty or so was a respected medical doctor. Her blue-green eyes appraised the monitor with seemingly cool detachment.

"Right," the on-screen doctor said. "That's exactly right."

"Both indicate lysosomal storage illness."

"They do." The doctor seemed slightly taken aback, her thunder stolen. "You're the boy's primary physician, Dr., uh—"

"Scully. Dana Scully."

"Dr. Scully, yes. And you tested the lysosome functions?"

"I think you have all my results there. Should be complete."

The doctor on the flat screen began shuffling through her paperwork. *Had the woman not given the material proper attention?* Scully wondered.

"My fear," Scully said, her voice even, allowing no irritation with this high-paid consultant to show through, "is that it's a type two degenerative brain disease . . . like Sandhoff disease."

Though Scully need not refer to it, all this information was at her fingertips, within a notebook on the inside cover of which she'd taped a photograph of her patient, young Christian Fearon, so that whenever she had to glance at the cold, hard medical facts, she would first see the six-year-old's upbeat, smiling face. The photo was signed: *For Dr. Scully. Love, Christian.*

"I'm concerned," Scully said, "that my patient's enzymes aren't clearing lipids from his brain, causing atrophy, and—"

"If you suspect Sandhoff disease," the head on the screen cut in, "I would test the boy's levels of hexosaminidase . . ."

"I've done that, of course. What I'm really looking for, Doctor, is a course of treatment."

"There is no course of treatment for Sandhoff disease."

The reply, from the doctor on satellite, had been abrupt, even cold. And this was not the response Scully had hoped for, from so highly regarded a consultant. For a moment her professional facade dropped, and the caring woman showed through.

Not that the head on the screen felt any empathy, only adding a prickly, "But if there *were* a treatment, Dr. Scully, I'm quite sure you'd tell me."

That was uncalled for, though Scully made no response. Such small concerns as reminding their electronic guest that a consultation of this kind should include common courtesy—and that any clash of egos was inappropriate—had vanished within Scully. She felt as though she'd been struck a blow to the belly, as if all the air in her, like her hopes, had gone whooshing out.

The eyes of her colleagues were on her. These men and women knew Scully as a scientifically minded, coolly objective professional, and the humanity she'd betrayed, the emotions beneath the normally self-composed surface, surprised them.

But no face betrayed that surprise more obviously than that of Father Ybarra, the priest who was the venerable hospital's top administrator.

She managed to thank the on-screen doctor for sharing her expertise, gathered the notebook, and got up from the table.

"Dana," Father Ybarra said, still seated.

She paused at the door.

He rose, a tall, almost skeletal man in his mid-forties whose long sorrowful face held kind eyes. "I know you must be disappointed. You know I'll say a prayer for your young patient."

"So will I, Father. But I'm not quite ready to leave his fate to God."

She did her best not to stumble out of the conference room. She could feel Ybarra's eyes on her, following her out, but he himself did not, for which Scully was grateful.

In the corridor of the old hospital, moving past

several nuns, Scully headed back toward her office, movement itself burdensome under the weight of the outside expert's opinion. Before she reached her destination, her head lowered as she fought the miasma of disappointment, Scully almost bumped into the very family she hoped to help.

Margaret and Blair Fearon, a salt-of-the-earth working-class couple in their late twenties who deserved better, were rolling their young son Christian down the hall in his wheelchair. Blair, lanky and brown-haired, towered over wife Margaret, a pretty redhead. The hopeful faces of the parents found Scully's, and she instantly covered her despair with confidence.

As for Christian, the frail boy in the elephants-and-clowns hospital gown gave her a smile as radiant as it was lopsided—his brain cancer, ever worsening, had made it hard for him to express himself.

She bent slightly as she smiled at the child, saying, "Hi, Christian. How are you feeling?"

"Okay, Dr. Scully," he said, each word an effort, but one he seemed to think worthwhile. "How are you?"

"Me? I'm doing just fine."

"You look pretty."

"Thank you, Christian. Nice to hear from a handsome young man." Her eyes lifted to meet the beseeching expressions of Christian's parents; their hope was almost as hard to take as that callous consultant's words.

These young parents had aged ten years in the months Scully had known them; they had the haggard look of refugees, and why not? Weren't they after all casualties in this most personal of wars?

Blair Fearon risked a smile. "Dr. Scully, did you get some outside opinions?"

"Yes." She grasped the notebook Christian had given her, as if it were keeping her afloat. "I just came from a satellite consultation."

"Good news?"

She tilted her head. "Forward movement. We're going to start by doing more tests."

The eyes of the parents died a little. Looking up at her from his chair, Christian stayed ever sunny, even though this child had suffered more than his share of hospital horrors.

"Dr. Scully," Margaret said, "Christian's already been through dozens of tests. Isn't it time to start treating this illness, *really* treating it?"

"Soon," Scully said, and her tight smile was meant to give them a few rays of hope, yet not build them up too much. "The next round of tests should point the way for us."

"*Dana Scully . . .*"

The voice behind her hadn't posed a question. If anything, it was an order, an order to turn around and see what this sonorous voice wanted.

And when despite herself she complied, Scully knew at once who she was looking at, though she had never seen this commanding, unsmiling African American before, a man of perhaps thirty-five, a rugged six feet packaged in a crisp navy-blue suit with a blue dress shirt and a perfectly knotted black-striped-blue tie.

It was that suit, added to the tone of voice, that told her she was facing an FBI agent.

"Dr. Scully," he said, "I'm looking for Fox Mulder."

She smiled at the little family, excused herself, and moved off, and her tall, broad-shouldered visitor followed along.

"I'm Special Agent Mosley Drummy," he said. "With—"

"I can guess who you're with." She continued down the corridor as he kept up. "You're with people who've been looking for Fox Mulder for a long time."

His manner was brusque, businesslike. "Old sins can be forgiven. Charges can be expunged."

"Under what circumstances?"

Drummy did something with his lips that wasn't quite a smile. "The FBI needs urgently to speak with Fox Mulder. They're hoping you can help them."

She stopped abruptly and so did the agent. They faced each other.

"You don't understand," she said. "I don't work

with Fox Mulder any longer. And I don't work with the FBI, either. Forensics pathology is my past. I work with the living now."

Drummy said, "Good. Because if there's any way you could contact Mulder, it might save a life."

She said nothing, but could not hide her interest.

"The life of an *FBI agent*, Dr. Scully."

She studied the hard, chiseled features. Drummy's eyes were unreadable, but that was no surprise—it came with the badge and gun. His words, however, carried an undercurrent of concern. An agent's life was at stake, and SA Mosley Drummy worked with that agent. That Scully would bet on.

But could she safely bet that the FBI wasn't playing her? That those old sins, those old charges, would be anything but expunged or forgiven?

And would Dana Scully wind up the Judas sheep for Fox Mulder?

Rural Virginia
January 9

Dusk had not quite arrived when Dana Scully guided her white Taurus down a two-lane highway through a snow-covered landscape suitable for a Currier and Ives print. But by the time she pulled into an unmarked lane blocked by a paint-peeling metal gate, anything picturesque about the drive had faded with the day.

She left the car running as she got out, walked to the gate, and unlocked it. Her eyes could not keep themselves from checking if she was being watched as she swung the gate open, got back in her car, and nosed in just clear of the gate. Again she left the car, this time closed the gate, reached around and locked it again, with her eyes traveling everywhere in that old suspicious manner, a habit that over the years and months had gradually gone away.

Till now.

She and the Taurus made their way down the bumpy, snow-patched gravel road until they came to a dreary little low-slung, single-story house. Unremarkable in every way, the small clapboard might appear abandoned, if a few lights had not been on within.

The interior—after she unlocked the front door and stepped in, putting her valise on a table—did not have the desolate look of the exterior. This was a homey place, lived in, with furniture that was either secondhand or had been around long enough to seem to be. She took off her long tan cashmere topcoat, revealing a dark blue silk blouse and tailored blue slacks, looking too chic by half for these modest surroundings. But she did in fact live here. She hung up the coat in the closet and moved through the little living room to a hallway, where she opened a door.

The room, a small converted bedroom, reminded her of the cramped office in the bowels of the FBI Building where she and Fox Mulder had once worked on X-Files cases, those unexplained crimes and events that had been designated X and consigned to a sort of bureaucratic scrap heap, till Mulder—the young hotshot from Violent Crimes—had taken an interest.

Here, in this spare bedroom of the small clapboard house, were walls arrayed with photographs and clippings detailing sundry strange phenomena and images of UFOs and monsters from Bigfoot to lake creatures to little green men. Even the inside of the door was covered with such flotsam and jetsam of American life, snipped out of newspapers and magazines or printed off the Internet, stories of conspiracy theories and ETs and supposed supernatural happenings. This was the office or den or perhaps lair of a true obsessive.

She had been in the doorway only a moment, his back to her as he sat at his desk, when he said, "What's up, Doc?"

"You've become awfully trusting, Mulder," she said, smirking, "for a man wanted by the FBI. What if I'd been someone else?"

Fox Mulder, a fugitive in a gray sweater and jeans, still did not turn; but she knew what he was doing: clipping an item from a newspaper. Mulder subscribed to thirty newspapers and magazines and kept a P.O. box in Richmond for just that purpose.

He said, "Eyes in the back of my head, Scully," snipping away.

She folded her arms, leaned against the doorjamb. Some things never changed. Mulder was one of them.

"*Auf einer wellenlange*, the Germans say," he said in that dry yet lilting way of his. "A precognitive state, Scully, often confused with simple human intuition . . . you *have* heard of woman's intuition? . . . in which the brain perceives the deep logic of transitory existence unaided by the rational mind."

She gaped at his back. So now "eyes in the back of the head" was a scientifically proven paranormal gift? My God, he could go on. After all these years, he could still go on . . .

"Moments of clarity," he continued, still clipping, "materializing as conscious awareness of space and time independent from all sensible reality."

She shook her head for her own benefit. As if "sensible reality" were anything Mulder knew a damn thing about.

He laid the clipping out carefully on a desk that seemed cluttered but wasn't, method in his madness. The major obstacle was the abundance of sunflower-seed shells overflowing their dish, awaiting their turn in a wastebasket rife with them.

Then he swiveled to her. Despite his full growth of facial hair, and his forty-some years on the planet, he still had a youthful countenance, including those puppy-dog hazel eyes. And though he'd buried himself in this office for . . . how many years now? . . . she still could see in him that childlike sense of wonder.

Some days, anyway.

Mulder lifted a finger, gently lecturing up at her. "Such moments of clarity can materialize much as you just did, Scully. Though if you'd actually 'materialized,' you'd likely be rapidly dematerializing by now."

She raised her arms and her eyebrows. *See? I'm still here . . .*

Mulder's eyes lost some spark, going half-lidded. "But who believes that crap anymore?"

As if to prove his point, Mulder rose and went over to pin the clipping on the wall, close enough for Scully to read the headline: PRINCETON CLOSES ESP LAB AFTER 40 YEARS OF PARANORMAL STUDY. Well, not on the wall, onto a poster on the wall, an image of a flying saucer in a blue sky over trees, a poster that had been prominent in their basement office at the FBI and that Scully had come to identify with her partner: I WANT TO BELIEVE.

A poster that seemed dog-eared now, ancient history and not a cry to battle.

Scully said, "You still believe."

"Do I?"

"Even if not . . . someone does at the FBI, apparently."

Half a smile made itself known in the nest of beard. But it faded as Mulder studied Scully's straight face.

She said, "I had a visitor at the hospital today."

His eyes tightened. "I don't like the sound of this."

"The FBI wants your help, Mulder. To find a missing agent."

Now the eyes widened. "Tell me you said go screw yourselves. You know as well as I do, Scully, they'd rather see me dead and buried."

He went back to his chair and sat down again. She pulled up another chair and leaned in and touched his arm.

"They say all is forgiven," she said. "And they'll drop any charges against you, if you'll just come in and help them solve this one case."

Now his eyes flared. "The FBI will forgive *me*? How about, will I forgive the FBI for putting me on trial, on bogus charges, and trying to discredit a decade of my work? Of *our* work."

"Mulder . . ."

"They should be asking *me* for *my* forgiveness."

She locked eyes with him. "I think they are, Mulder. Desperately."

He shrugged. "How could I possibly help these people?"

"It's an X-File, Mulder."

"There is no X-Files."

"There *are* X-Files, just no agents handling them."

He said nothing for a few moments, then: "Is Skinner involved?"

Walter Skinner, the assistant director of the FBI, had been their friend and ally over the years, even in the darkest days.

"No. The ASAC is Dakota Whitney."

"Don't know her."

Scully shrugged. "I don't, either. The agent who came to see me, Mosley Drummy, I also don't know."

"That's comforting." His sigh was more disgusted than weary. "Why *me*, Scully?"

"There's someone who's come forward with promising evidence about this missing agent. A psychic, or so he claims."

Mulder shook his head. "It's a trick, Scully. To smoke me out."

And she shook hers. "If the FBI really wanted to get you, Mulder, I've no doubt they could. I think they've been happy just having you out of their hair."

"Good. I'm happy to have them out of mine." His eyebrows rose. "Do the words *lethal injection* ring a bell?"

That stopped her for a moment. Then: "How long have we been living here, Mulder? In this house?"

"I don't know exactly. Five years?"

"Would Skinner have told me I could return to my career if we weren't safe? It's what we've always said—short of killing you? Your apprehension, with all the media attention it would bring, would do nothing but embarrass the bureau. And the government."

He raised a finger. "Let's go over that short-of-killing-you part again, Scully."

She gestured with both hands at the walls of clippings around them. "Wouldn't you like to step out into the sunshine again, Mulder? Wouldn't it be nice if we *both* could? Together?"

He swiveled his chair away from her.

She said, "There's a young agent's life at stake."

He shrugged, held up his hands, as if to say, *Not my problem*.

"Mulder . . . I know I don't have to say it, but . . . this could easily be you . . . or me . . . missing out there somewhere."

Mulder scratched his beard. His eyes searched his desk for something or other.

She shifted her tone. "Truth is, Mulder, I worry about you. And the effects of long-term isolation."

"I'm fine, Scully. Happy as a clam here."

"Really." She cast her eyes toward the ceiling, where in the tiles were stuck dozens of pencils, tossed up there in nervous frustration by the bearded man at the desk.

She rose. "I tried . . . I'll let them know your answer."

She didn't pause at the door, just went on out into the living room, not seeing the man she shared this house with, her life with, sitting thinking at the desk. And swiveling to cast his eyes on the poster, and those familiar words: I WANT TO BELIEVE.

She did, however, hear him when he said quietly: "I'll go."

She turned and he was in his doorway. His expression was deadpan, but something in his eyes told her that she'd won, although she wasn't sure that was a good thing.

"On one condition," he said.

She smiled. She knew what that condition was.

"All right," she said. "I'll go, too."

Chapter 3 _____

Washington, D.C.
January 9

From the helicopter, the abstraction that was his nation's capital city at night could thrill Fox Mulder as much as the next American. He was enough of a patriot to marvel at the familiar shapes of illuminated monuments rising with all their mythic power out of the light-dotted darkness. He was enough of a romantic to hope that the greatness of the American dream could still come true, despite all the nightmares he'd witnessed.

But the nightmares could not be dismissed. Seated by Scully in the FBI chopper, cold despite the brown topcoat he'd flung over his sweater and jeans, Mulder could only look over at his former

X-Files partner, and forever life partner, and think how small she seemed, how vulnerable, despite his knowledge of just how strong in every way this petite woman could be. She had talked him into this, but his insistence that she go, too, had put her in the seat next to him, and her expression told him that she shared with him the same apprehensions about their impending homecoming.

As the aircraft slowed over Pennsylvania Avenue to descend over the familiar, triangular-shaped J. Edgar Hoover FBI Building, with its severe lines and beehive of windows, Mulder smiled at Scully and said, somehow working his voice up over the churning chopper blades, "If it's a trap, I'll make a break for it. You cover me."

She just gave him that pursed-lip look, that cross between a kiss and a smirk he knew so well.

When they stepped from the chopper onto the rooftop, a tall African American in a navy suit awaited them, the artificial wind of the helicopter flapping the man's clothes and making a waving flag of his tie. He appeared supremely bored. This would be Scully's hospital contact, Special Agent Drummy.

Mulder approached the agent, who offered no greetings, and said, "Thanks for the lift. Wouldn't want to hitch on a night like this."

"Don't thank me," Drummy said, eyes as cold as the weather around them. "*I* didn't send it."

Mulder glanced at Scully, who frowned just a little. The cold shoulder from the guy who'd invited them? What was that about? Right now SA Drummy was moving ahead of them, toward the doors into the building, and the two former FBI agents followed dutifully, if for no other reason than to come in from the cold.

Come in from the cold is right, Mulder thought.

This time of night, even a bustling enterprise like the FBI Building was fairly deserted. Drummy was keeping a brisk pace, and Mulder and Scully, side by side, followed a few steps behind, traversing several gray corridors. They were both in civvies—Scully in her camel-hair topcoat over a light blue blouse and darker slacks—and the few agents they did pass gave them suspicious glances.

Scully seemed vaguely offended. "They're looking at us like suspects."

He smiled a little. "Aren't we?"

Finally Drummy, his eyes as cold in the warmth of the building as they'd been on the chilly rooftop, paused at a doorway. He said, "Wait here," opened the door, letting out the noise of busy worker bees, then went in and shut it hard—not quite a slam but a nice period for the end of his sentence.

Mulder and Scully stood there alone.

Mulder said, "I think he likes you."

"I don't know what his problem is."

"Just shy."

Scully was glancing at the framed photo of J. Edgar Hoover on one wall, while Mulder noticed a similar portrait of George W. Bush. The last time Mulder had been in this building, the current president had just come into office; now Mulder was back and that president would before long be on his way out. He and Scully no longer belonged here and yet they did, ghosts haunting their own former, well, haunts.

Drummy's impassive, vaguely sullen countenance stuck itself out of the doorway.

Mulder managed not to say, *Joe sent me.*

Drummy said, "Come in."

Mulder and Scully stepped into the sort of conference room they'd been in countless times before, though not always finding this current state of heavy activity—this was a provisional command post, with a controlled turmoil all too familiar to the couple, as a dozen FBI agents sat around the conference table, working phones, hunkered at laptops, taking notes, with others up at wall-mounted bulletin boards with photos and maps tacked on.

These law enforcement professionals had barely slept for days, existing on coffee and carryout, as the heavy beards on the men and the scant makeup on the women, and the bloodshot eyes all around, indicated. The arrival of two former agents, sent for as part of this endeavor, elicited no greetings, not even smiles, nothing to indicate that Mulder and Scully indeed weren't ghosts haunting their former workplace.

Two trimly professional-looking women across the room were locked in conversation, one handsome if severe in a white blouse and black suit, the other a slender, beautiful brunette also in simple, stylish black, her hair ponytailed back. As Mulder and Scully lingered near the entrance, this conversation continued, and a few glances from the severe woman gave Mulder the impression that neither he nor Scully was loved.

But then the conversation broke off, and the brunette with the ponytail came toward them and offered Scully a businesslike smile and her hand. As the two women shook, the brunette said, "Thanks for making this happen. I'm Assistant Special Agent in Charge Whitney."

This was directed to Scully, who nonetheless identified herself: "Dana Scully."

Whitney, direct and pleasant, turned to Mulder and extended a hand. "Fox Mulder, I believe."

He took her hand, with just a twinge of suspicion. With that woman across the room still casting the occasional seeming look of disapproval, Mulder would not have been surprised if a handcuff were snapped down his wrist.

"*Assistant* Special Agent?" Mulder said. "You *are* in charge of this investigation?"

"I am," she said with a crisp nod. The narrow

oval of her face held lovely features, in particular striking light blue eyes. "I know this is awkward, Agent Mulder—"

"Not 'agent' anymore. Just Mulder. And Scully."

Another crisp nod. "Well, in any event, welcome back to the bureau. My team and I appreciate your trust." She was reaching for a file on the nearby table. Mulder, guarded though he was, already liked her—she had a disarming manner, and wasted no energy.

"Trust being what it is," Mulder said, "what happens if I can't help? Or your agent turns up dead? I'm not exactly in a position to guarantee my work, Agent Whitney."

She shook her head. "The past is the past. We know your work on X-File cases here and believe you may be the best chance Monica Bannan has right now."

"Chance of what?"

"Not to die, Mulder. Not to die." She handed him the file.

He opened it and saw a head shot of a woman who was perhaps thirty, nose rather prominent, features sharp but in a not unattractive way.

Scully asked, "How long has she been missing?"

"Since Sunday evening," Whitney said. "Almost three days."

Scully and Mulder traded quick dark looks. Then Mulder's gaze returned to the photo of the missing woman, while Scully said, "Agent Whitney, I know you know this . . . but there's slim chance, after seventy-two hours, that she's still alive."

Whitney's nod was as curt as it was reluctant. "And we have slim reason to believe she is, that's true. But so far we've got no evidence to the contrary, either. And the facts we do have give us hope."

The ASAC plucked another file from the table and handed this one to Scully, who opened it and saw several photos, taken in a lab setting, of an arm—a severed or perhaps amputated human arm with a jagged wound near the wrist.

"Soon after Agent Bannan went missing," Whitney said, indicating the arm in the photo, "we found that."

Mulder looked up from the agent's photo. "Where?"

"About ten miles from her home."

Scully was frowning. "I don't understand. That's a *man's* arm . . ."

"A man's arm," Mulder said softly, matter-of-fact, eyes flicking from Scully to Whitney, "that's a match for evidence your team found at or near the crime scene. Blood or tissue."

Whitney shot a look at the table of agents, some of whom were eavesdropping, including that severely handsome woman in black. It was as if the ASAC had said, *See? Told you. He's good.*

Then Whitney said, "Blood found near Monica

Bannan's carport, and on a gardening tool there, matches that wound."

Scully's eyes flared. "And this is what you're basing your hopes on?"

Whitney took that placidly. "Agent Bannan's service weapon was locked in the trunk of her car; she had another gun, but in the house. That wound, matching that tool, could be evidence that Monica Bannan fought back. She was most certainly trained and able to."

Mulder nodded, barely. Referring to the severed arm, he asked, "What did forensics say about it?"

Shaking her head, Whitney said, "Male, thirty-five to forty. No match in CODIS for prints."

By now Mulder had put together why he was here; he imagined Scully had, too. "I take it you were led to that detached arm like . . ."

"A needle in a haystack," Whitney said.

"I was thinking more, a needle in a stack of needles." Mulder glanced at Scully, then said to the ASAC: "You were led there by someone claiming psychic powers."

Whitney's nod was slow this time. "Joseph Patrick Crissman."

Mulder twitched a smile. "And you think he's full of shit."

Agent Drummy, listening nearby, traded his deadpan for a smirk, and said to Mulder, "What makes you say that?"

Mulder knew how to turn a deadpan into a smirk, too. "Maybe *I'm* psychic."

"Look," Drummy said, lumbering over. "This guy, this Father Joe—"

"*Father?*" Scully said, head tilted, eyes narrowed. "He's a *priest*?"

Drummy shrugged. "Catholic."

Mulder glanced at Scully, and, right on cue, a little light from above winked off the little gold cross around her neck. Fluorescent light from above, anyway.

Scully said, "*He* contacted *you*?"

Drummy nodded. "He cold-calls us six hours after Agent Bannan's reported missing. At that point, nothing had been in the media, understand. We were still sitting on it. And here he is claiming he saw a vision of her. Claiming he has a psychic connection."

Mulder said, "And Father Joe tells you Monica Bannan is alive."

"That's right," Drummy said.

"Claiming a psychic connection. But have you found any *other* connection?"

"To Monica Bannan?"

That was one of those dumb questions that deserved a wisecrack, and Mulder was choosing between several options when ASAC Whitney said, "No. No connection. And that's why I sent for you."

Mulder glanced at Scully; the smile they exchanged was so small, no one but each other would have spotted it. But they both understood Agent Drummy's attitude now: Mulder was a threat. Drummy was a by-the-book agent, and old Spooky Mulder from the X-Files was getting hauled in to do his stuff and maybe make Drummy look like an unimaginative also-ran.

Whitney was saying, "I need your expert opinion, Mulder. I need to know we're not wasting time, going down this route. Because we don't have time to waste."

"Not," Scully said dryly, "after seventy-two hours."

Mulder nodded, weighing the facts . . . and the past . . . and the politics. Getting involved here was dangerous. Even being back in this building was crazy. But somewhere a missing FBI agent was in trouble. As he had been, so many times. And Scully.

Then he said, "We're talking about a religious man, clearly. Well-educated man. He took the right action, as he saw it, and called you, saying nothing to cast doubt upon himself or his motives. He has no material connection to the crime. You *are* wasting time, Agent Whitney."

That startled her, the blue eyes popping. "What?"

"Only the time you're wasting is *mine* . . . and all these agents'." He locked eyes with her. "Go down this route now. It's all you have and there's no reason to doubt him."

"Look," Whitney said, "there's a question of credibility . . ."

"If you have no good reason to doubt him, why doubt the man's visions?"

Frowning, Drummy broke in: "Listen, Mulder, he didn't lead us to Monica Bannan, okay? He gave us some guy's bloody arm in the snow!"

Mulder's shoulders came up and then went down. "Hey, it's not an exact science. If it were me, running this case? I'd be sticking with this guy round the clock. I'd be in bed with him, kissing his holy ass."

Scully closed her eyes. The agents at the conference table, who'd been watching with various degrees of skepticism and distrust, seemed openly contemptuous now.

Whitney said, "Mulder—Father Joe is a convicted pedophile."

Scully's eyes opened. She trained them right on Mulder, as surprised as he was.

"Maybe," Mulder said, "I'd stay out of bed with him."

Richmond, Virginia
January 9

Two black Ford Expeditions drew up to a stop in front of an apartment complex that was distinguished from the surrounding residential neighborhood only by the starkness of its lines and the brightness of its exterior lighting. Pale cement walls cut by the black of metal stairs gave the place an almost prisonlike look. Or was Mulder just reading in, knowing who lived here?

Mulder and Scully got out of the back of the lead SUV and followed ASAC Whitney and SA Drummy as they made their way down the sidewalk past skimpy, skeletal trees through a flat snowy yard, breaths visible in the chill.

Scully fell in alongside Whitney, Mulder trailing.

"What *is* this place?" Scully asked.

Whitney, her voice flat, said, "Dorms for habitual sex offenders."

"Dorms?"

"They manage the complex and police themselves. Father Joe lives here voluntarily, with his roommate."

Scully looked like she was tasting something foul, and Mulder gave her his best boyish smile. "Might want to avoid the activities room."

And they moved into the stark complex.

Soon they were in a hallway that could have led to a parking ramp but instead brought them to a cold corridor of doors, at one of which they stopped. Drummy knocked as Whitney, Scully, and Mulder looked uncomfortably on. Moments passed while, presumably, someone checked them out via a peephole.

Mulder said to Scully softly, "Can't be too careful."

Scully didn't seem to be in the mood for levity.

The door opened, and a slight, fiftyish man with a long, sorrowful face filled the frame. He wore a corduroy jacket and a striped polo shirt with brown woolen trousers and looked about as threatening as your favorite uncle. But then favorite uncles could be pretty threatening, Mulder knew, if yours was a sexual predator and you were a little boy or girl.

The slight man spoke, not to them, but to someone behind him: "Joe . . ."

The response came from deep in the apartment in a second tenor touched with a Scottish accent that gave it a certain musical quality: "Tell them to come in!"

The four callers trooped into a modest, somewhat sloppy living area hanging with the stench of heavy cigarette use and the overflowing ashtrays to prove it. The decor was Early Goodwill, magazines and newspapers stacked here and there, a tube TV playing an ancient rerun of *The Jeffersons*. Probably the start or finish of an episode, Mulder noted, as the theme song—"Movin' On Up"—was playing, though the tenants of this apartment sure weren't going anywhere.

The threadbare couch and a shabby recliner

were vacant, the living room itself lit mostly by the glow of the television and a single floor lamp; but through a cracked door onto a bedroom, Mulder could see a man in his sixties in patchwork-print robe, T-shirt, and gray flannel trousers, kneeling on the floor, saying his rosary. The man's hair was a wild tangle of gray and some black, and his long face was made longer by a goatee.

Drummy identified the man for Mulder and Scully, by speaking to him at the cracked door: "Father Joe? A word?"

Even the Lord God was subject to Drummy's sullen impatience.

Mulder watched the ex-priest rise, and then the door opened all the way and Joseph Crissman emerged, mumbling, "Excuse the mess . . ."

The old boy had been smoking as he prayed and he now stubbed out a mostly gone cigarette in an overflowing ashtray. Then he found the television remote and turned down the antics of the Jefferson family.

He shrugged, said, "I haven't been sleeping," as if to answer a question he hadn't been asked, and trundled absently past Scully, brushing by her, and began to halfheartedly straighten things on the couch, making room for his guests, though no one made a move to sit down.

Mulder studied their host, who seemed to be half sleepwalking.

Drummy, fighting irritation (no surprise), said, "Father Joe, this is Fox Mulder."

Crissman glanced Mulder's way and seemed to look through him. "Okay," he said.

No argument. Mulder was Mulder. Next.

"He'd like to ask you some questions—"

"Actually," Scully said, stepping forward, "*I* want to ask something."

Mulder knew that chip-on-her-shoulder tone all too well. Whitney and Drummy turned to her, recognizing strained indignation when they heard it.

"I just saw you praying," Scully said, facing him. "What were you praying for, in there . . . sir?"

Father Joe, easily over six feet, loomed over the petite Scully, not that she seemed to give a damn. His eyes lost their preoccupation and stared right at her, then fell to the necklace and its gold cross.

"I was praying," he said evenly, his eyes returning to her face, "for the salvation of my immortal soul."

She nodded appraisingly. "And you believe that God hears your prayers?"

Crissman almost smiled. Almost. "Do you believe He hears *yours*?"

"There are no young screams getting in the way." Her arms were folded, her head cocked, her voice steady. "You see, I didn't bugger thirty-seven altar boys."

Mulder managed not to chuckle while the two

FBI agents had that clubbed-baby-seal look that Scully could inspire in those who didn't know how outspoken she could be.

Mulder said to her, conversationally, "Interesting way to put it."

"I have another word," she said, "if you'd like."

"No. It's okay. I follow."

But if Father Crissman followed, he showed no sign of it. The old boy hadn't flinched. And now he merely plopped himself down on the sofa and reached for a pack of cigarettes as he coughed his smoker's cough. *Wasn't suicide itself a sin?* Mulder thought. He'd have to ask Scully later if smoking counted.

"Young lady," he said to Scully, as he selected a smoke, "I have to believe He does hear me. Or else why would He be sending me these visions?"

Scully took a step toward him. "Maybe it's not God doing the sending."

He turned a hand. "But the first one came during Communion, my dear."

Mulder could feel the hatred coming off Scully like heat; and the ex-priest's arrogance was just as palpable.

Casually, Mulder said, "You call them visions. You *see* them, then?"

Crissman nodded. "In what you might call . . . my mind's eye."

The Scottish burr was strangely lulling.

Mulder asked, "What do you see exactly?"

Crissman was lighting his cigarette. He inhaled deeply, taking his own good time to exhale. Mulder knew this character liked center stage, which was neither a good sign nor a bad one: Plenty of genuine psychics were also unrepentant hams.

"I see," Crissman said, as if he were reading off a grocery list, "the poor girl being assaulted. I see her fighting back. I see a bloody arm . . ."

Mulder pressed: "*Where* do you see her?"

The father shook his head. "I don't know. I hear dogs barking."

From the way Whitney and Drummy exchanged glances, Mulder realized this was a new piece of information. But Scully picked up on that, too, and her glance at Mulder somehow underscored that this latest detail seemed suspiciously random.

Whitney stepped up. "*Where*, Father Joe? Where are these barking dogs?"

A shrug. A shake of the head. "I can't tell."

"But you see her *alive*?"

"No."

Mulder could see the air go out of Whitney.

Then the ex-priest said, "But I . . . *feel* that she is still with us."

Mulder asked, "Can you show us how you do it?"

Crissman took another deep drag off his cigarette, rested it in the ashtray, then closed his eyes. Scully gave Mulder an *oh-brother!* look.

"I don't know," Father Joe said, "that I can do it right now."

Scully was shaking her head; whatever shreds of patience she had left were clearly falling away. But when she returned her eyes to Crissman's, his gaze was fixed upon her.

"Maybe I'd do better," Crissman said coldly, nodding toward Scully, "if *she* weren't here."

Scully's eyes narrowed. "Maybe what you 'see' is a way to make people forget what you *really* are."

Then she turned and stalked out of the apartment.

Mulder was torn—he should follow her. But Scully wouldn't be going far, and he still didn't have a handle on Father Joe here. He would stay and ask a few more questions.

After all, his being here was Scully's idea, wasn't it?

Chapter 4 _____

Dana Scully, in the cold concrete corridor of what ASAC Dakota Whitney had described as a "dorm" for sex offenders, stood studying the FBI file. Specifically, she concentrated on the photos of the severed arm found in the snow, where "Father" Joe Crissman had led them.

The apartment door opened and Scully looked up, expecting to see Mulder, but instead saw Crissman's slight, pale roommate, exiting on his way somewhere. His haunted eyes went to her face, but she lowered her view, returning to the grotesque images of the detached arm with its gouged flesh near the wrist.

Someone touched her own arm, and she jumped a little, whirling to face Mulder.

"Jesus, Mulder!" she said. "Talk about materializing."

He half smiled. "And so much for kissing our psychic's holy ass."

"You believe him?"

"I don't know. I don't know."

Suddenly embarrassed, Scully said, "I'm sorry. I . . . I've been away from this business too long." She rolled her eyes. "Or maybe not long enough."

But Mulder was shaking his head. "No, you were good in there, Scully."

She gave him the you-can't-be-serious look.

"All I had were questions," Mulder said. "You went after him. You challenged him. Like old times."

She liked hearing that but tried not to show it, saying, "Yeah, well, he's a creep. And a liar. Mulder, he knows who did this, and the abductors are supplying him with information."

"How would an ex-priest know these criminals?"

"Look where he lives!" She handed him the file with its photos and in particular the last shot she'd been studying. "This arm that they found—it wasn't severed in a fight with Monica Bannan or anybody else. It was *chopped* off, Mulder."

He frowned at the photo.

Scully went on: "*Cleanly*, judging by that photo.

That's an amputation, not a casualty of war. And tell me how the good father leads them straight to it, when he can't even muster a *guess* where the victim is?"

Mulder said nothing.

Scully said, "Two things they'll find in the next twenty-four hours: a dead FBI agent, and that this 'psychic,' this 'Father' Joe, is a big, fat fraud."

Mulder's eyes rose from the photo to Scully. He had that blank look that could elicit in her both love and frustration, among half a dozen other emotions.

He gave her a tiny shrug and said, "You could be right, Scully."

Behind them, the apartment door opened and ASAC Whitney and SA Drummy filed out. Bringing up the rear was Father Joe himself, fully dressed now, a gray tweed jacket over a sweater, heavy gray trousers and black snow boots; the man was tugging on brown leather gloves and did not look their way. The little contingent moved down the corridor, presumably toward where the Expeditions were parked.

Her eyes went from the group back to Mulder's face. "Tell me you're not part of this . . ."

"What if you're wrong, Scully? What if Father Joe is Agent Bannan's one best chance?"

He started down the hallway after them, and Scully, wide-eyed, fell in alongside him.

"Mulder, what are you *doing*?"

"We're taking him for a ride. So we can see just how psychic Father Joe really is."

She paused and so did he. She sighed. Her eyes closed, and when they opened they were still half-lidded. "Yeah, well. It's been fun."

They walked back down to where the Expeditions awaited. At one point, Father Joe came close enough to Scully to give her a shudder. Mulder caught that and touched her shoulder.

He said, gently, "No one's gonna make you sit with him."

But Scully was already shaking her head. "Thanks, but I've already been taken for a ride tonight. Anyway, Crissman made it clear—he doesn't want me here. I interfere with his process. Too much negativity."

Disgusted, she moved toward one of the parked vehicles, the one Father Joe was not climbing into, and Mulder stayed right with her.

"*I* want you here," he told her.

She opened the car door. "I'm going to be asked to be taken back home. You know, nothing says you have to be part of this, either."

"Scully . . ."

"This isn't my life anymore, Mulder. I'm done chasing after monsters in the night; I've gone into my last dark crime scene with a flashlight. I think you've done all they asked of you here, too. You don't have to stay."

Mulder swallowed, and nodded. He looked back at Whitney and Drummy, piling in the other Expedition with Crissman. She was reminded of a child wanting to go on a sleepover and Mommy was saying no. No sleepovers, not with the likes of Father Joe.

Nodding toward them, Mulder said, "These people need my help."

Was he echoing her own words back at her, to make a point, or was that just how it came out? Either way the irony was not lost on her.

"And, Scully—I could really use yours." He handed her back the FBI file. He was not asking her to come along, just to stay involved. To spend more time with the evidence. No monsters, no flashlights, just bring your expertise to the evidence. All of this Mulder said to her in one lingering look from those damn puppy-dog eyes of his.

She nodded, reluctantly, and took the file.

Rural Virginia
January 10

As the Expedition glided in darkness along the country road through a seemingly idyllic snowy vista, dawn turned the horizon pink behind lush firs and naked trees alike, the rest of the sky and the world below washed blue.

Fox Mulder was in the backseat next to Father

Joe Crissman, who leaned against the window, slumped in snoring sleep. SA Drummy was driving, ASAC Whitney riding shotgun, and now and then each agent would meet Mulder's eyes in the rearview mirror, always with the same unspoken question: *What the hell are we doing here?*

When the Expedition took a sizable bump, Father Joe was jolted awake with a snort.

His eyes startled under gray eyebrows, the ex-priest asked, "Are we getting warm?"

Whitney glanced over the shoulder of her black thermal jacket. "You tell us." Unspoken was: *You're the psychic, remember?*

Father Joe looked out the vehicle's every window. Still groggy from his nap, he said, "I don't have the faintest idea where we are."

Mulder said, "That's okay."

Father Joe's eyes went to Mulder, who gave him a small smile, even as the agents in front glanced at each other impatiently, clearly wondering if they were on a fool's errand.

Mulder took a small picture of Monica Bannan from the FBI folder and handed it to Father Joe, saying, "Everyone works differently. Take your time."

Father Joe appraised Mulder skeptically. "And what are you—the good cop?"

"I'm the non-cop."

The priest thought about that briefly, then fixed

his eyes on the photo of the missing agent. "I don't know this girl. I doubt we ever met. My contacts, as you surely must know, are rather limited these days. I don't have a clue, the connection."

"There's always something, however small," Mulder said. "Something that binds the two of you."

Father Joe was shaking his head. "So you *believe* in these sort of things?"

Mulder hesitated. He wanted to give the ex-priest enough support to encourage him, but needed to stop short of being an ally, much less his stooge.

"Let's just say," Mulder said softly, "I want to believe."

"Wants to believe," Drummy said from up in front, with casual contempt, "that his sister was abducted by aliens."

Mulder found Drummy's eyes in the rearview mirror and sent his own message of contempt, not so casual.

The priest asked, "Is that true?"

Mulder said nothing.

"Something you don't care to discuss?" Father Joe was studying Mulder's face. "A touchy subject, son?"

Mulder wasn't thrilled, being called "son" by a pedophile; but he said, "It was a long time ago."

They hit another bump.

"She's dead, isn't she?" The priest's features had

lost any trace of arrogance; nothing was in the man's expression but compassion. "Your sister?"

Lucky guess? Or was this wild-haired, wild-eyed former priest truly psychic?

Samantha was at peace now. Mulder knew this, believed it. He'd fought for so many years to find out the truth, and gone down countless false trails pursuing little green men and serial killers and impostors and even had seen his abduction memories discredited, but after all that and more, he had come to truly believe she was in a better place now. That she had been lost to him before his quest had really begun remained a frustration, but she was at peace and he was free of the need to try to save her. This did not mean he cared to have the likes of Drummy dismiss Samantha's memory, nor did he care to discuss his sister with a sex offender.

Mulder retrieved the photo of the missing agent from the priest's grasp, and his eyes went to the pleasant face of a young woman who might be alive or might be dead. Mulder did not see Whitney watching him in the rearview mirror, nor did he see the ASAC shift her attention to Father Joe, jumping a little because the man was staring right at her.

"This," the priest said, his voice shifting into a more commanding tone, "is where she was taken . . ."

Mulder glanced up from Agent Bannan's picture at Father Joe to find the man suddenly sitting forward, intense, cords standing out in his neck.

"*This*," the priest said, almost shouting, "*is where your agent was attacked!*"

Mulder found Whitney's eyes in the rearview mirror, and his expression asked her, *Is it?*

And hers replied: *Yes.*

Up ahead were the lights of a small housing development, looking yellow in the Maxfield Parrish blue of early morning.

Mulder said, "I want him to see the crime scene."

Drummy, at the wheel, exchanged a glance with Whitney; some hidden meaning was there, but Mulder couldn't find it. Not the contempt Drummy had shown him earlier. This was something else . . .

Soon the Expedition had turned off into the small settlement of single-story houses, then pulled up and stopped at the foot of an unplowed driveway. Drummy, putting up the hood of his black parka, came around to join Whitney. Mulder and Father Joe got out of the back just as the two FBI agents were heading up the snowy drive. Mulder fell in behind them and took half a dozen steps, his boots sinking deep, before he noticed the priest wasn't alongside him.

Mulder glanced back. Then, so did the agents.

Father Joe stood halfway up the driveway, frozen like a scarecrow against the blue sky.

"No," he said, shaking his head, strands of hair wiggling like Medusa's snakes. "It's . . . this isn't *right* . . ."

The big man in gray looked from side to side, as if trying to get his bearings. His eyes were unblinking and wide.

Then Crissman looked toward ASAC Whitney and said, frankly accusatory, with just a little of the Glasgow music, "You *brought* me to the wrong *house*."

And he turned and headed back down the drive and began crossing the road.

Mulder grinned back at the two agents. "Kinda pulled that one right outta his ass, huh?"

And Mulder followed.

So did the two agents.

The father's path angled across to another house where the carport was X'ed with yellow crime scene tape. Perhaps the priest had noticed that tape from the Expedition and they had just witnessed a little impromptu piece of theater. But Mulder didn't think so. After all, Mulder hadn't noticed. And he was paying attention.

Father Joe beat them there by half a minute, Mulder next to arrive, with Whitney and Drummy making a more tentative approach. The priest ducked under the wind-fluttered yellow tape and gazed at Monica Bannan's car, still parked there. Mulder ducked under the barrier, but, for the moment, the two agents kept their distance, their eyes glued to their would-be psychic.

Who was looking at all the right things—the driver's side door of the vehicle, the back wall of tools, from which Agent Bannan had surely selected a makeshift weapon, the path to the house where the struggle had begun. Agent Drummy came around to follow Father Joe, heading into the backyard.

Mulder sensed Whitney at his side and turned to her.

"Dis mus' be the place," Mulder said.

She shrugged. "There were news crews out here, covering the scene—pictures of the neighborhood. He could've recognized it from TV."

"Yes. But why?"

She blinked at him, those distinctive eyes a cool blue but nonetheless warm. "Why?" she echoed.

Mulder moved out from under the carport, watching as Agent Drummy followed Father Joe across the snowy landscape beyond the backyard, past which woods awaited that were about as inviting as what Snow White encountered.

"Why do it?" Mulder asked her. "Why go to such lengths and fabricate such an elaborate story?"

Whitney gave him a smile that said he was being naive—it was not unlike a couple thousand smiles Scully had given him.

"Expiation," she said. "Forgiveness of his sins."

"Father Joe thinks he can fool God?"

"Not God. He's written dozens of letters to the Vatican, pleading reengagement with the church."

Mulder's eyebrows went up and he half grinned. "Playing psychic to the FBI—rather odd way to impress the Holy See."

She shook her head. "Not really. Voice of God speaking through a man? That one's been a winner a few times."

"Got Joan of Arc burned at the stake. So you think he's a sham?"

She said nothing.

"You think he's *involved*? That he's guilty in this, somehow?"

Her eyes, like his, were on the two figures out on the snowy vista. "We have to consider him a suspect, yes."

"And yet you've found no connection to the crime."

She laughed, once. "Don't think my guys have stopped looking. They're turning over every stone in Father Joe Crissman's colorful life. And they think they're going to find something."

Mulder looked at her, engaged those blue eyes, realizing he'd been wrong just now. "But *you* don't—you think he's for real."

"Do I?"

"Yeah. Or I wouldn't be here."

She glanced at him. He could tell she was impressed by how he'd corralled her, clever devil that he was.

And when she spoke, something less professional and more human came in: "Let's just say I'm not the most popular girl at the FBI right now, for calling you in—believe me."

"You had me at FBI. Hey, I was Mr. Popular at

the bureau myself. You should see the storeroom they stuck me in. Spooky Mulder? Ring a bell?"

She smiled, shook her head; but her voice held undeniable respect, as she said, "You've dealt with psychics before—Luther Lee Boggs, Clyde Bruckman, Gerald Schnauz . . . I went through those cases, Mulder, and that work was extremely impressive."

"Yeah, well." He cocked his head. "I'm only half of the team, you know."

Her eyes narrowed. "You mean that, don't you? That's not false modesty."

"No. Scully keeps me honest. When she's not around, you better keep an eye on me."

"Okay." She smiled again. Lovely woman. "Understood. And Dana Scully's record is impressive, too. But it's *your* insights I need. Want to join the dance?"

So they headed out across the snow toward Drummy, who had planted himself and was watching Father Joe wander in the snow like a drunk looking for his car keys.

"This is ridiculous," Drummy said to Whitney.

She and Mulder were standing several yards away.

Mulder responded but not to Drummy, saying to Whitney, "No it isn't."

He was watching the priest, studying him the way a research doctor studies an organism on a slide.

"There's a specificity to his visions," Mulder said. "The straightforward way he presents them is a positive indicator. In my experience, most psychics are prone to dramatization, even if they're hot, and things are coming easily. They don't want it to *seem* too easy. So don't be put off by—"

Mulder stopped short. Both Whitney and Drummy, who'd been looking at their consultant, now followed Mulder's eyes to the priest, who was no longer wandering, and had stopped in one place.

And now, as if seized by an urge for prayer, Father Joe dropped to his knees.

Mulder began to run, his boots churning through the nearly knee-high snow; behind him, the two FBI agents were doing their best to keep up, footsteps crunching.

The priest, still on his knees, looked up at them as the three came to sudden, snow-stirring stops.

Crissman's features were even longer than usual, his eyes sorrowful, pain in every groove of his face. "She ran . . . she tried to escape." He looked to one side. "There were two men . . . but she couldn't . . ." His head came back to its original position. "He pushed her down! . . . Here." He nodded to the snow. "*Right here* . . . And then they put her in . . . in the back of . . ."

Whitney leaned forward, hands on her knees. "*Where?* Back of *what?*"

"In their car . . . no, a truck." His eyes did not

blink. He was looking straight ahead and yet seeing somewhere within him. "A truck with something . . . something *on* it." He squinted. "I don't know what . . ."

"We need more, Father," Whitney said desperately. "We need to *find* her . . ."

His face tightened. "She's in pain . . . in *great* pain . . ."

Whitney said, "Tell me *where*."

He shook his head. His eyes were half closed now. His expression seemed almost frightened. "I don't know. I can't see . . ."

"We have to *help* her. You have to *try* . . ."

But the shaggy-haired priest seemed near tears and approaching exhaustion. Again he shook his head. "I can't see . . . I can't *see* . . ."

Then the priest, still on his knees, fell onto his gloved hands and began to weep, deep, wrenching, racking sobs emerging from the depth of his being, even of his soul.

Drummy gave Mulder a dubious look, and all Mulder could think was how he wished Scully were there. He could be a sucker for a good act like this, but Scully would see through it, *if* it could be seen through, anyway. She would point out exactly what made it phony. If it were phony.

If she were here.

Drummy said, "You were right before, Mulder."

"Huh?"

"SOB does pull this shit right outta his ass."

Disgusted, the black agent wheeled and marched off through the deep snow.

But Mulder and Whitney remained, watching Father Joe, whose sobs continued and who seemed more and more to be just a melodramatic faker whose latest performance was going way over the top.

That was when Mulder saw the blood.

The drops of blood, dripping and plopping and puddling on the snow under Father Joe's hanging head.

Mulder stepped forward, put a hand on the man's nearer shoulder, and said, "Father? Are you—"

The big man with the wild hair gazed up at Mulder, who was taken aback by what he saw.

Father Joseph Crissman was weeping, all right. He wasn't faking. He really was crying.

Crying blood, red streaking his cheeks where the tears had trailed.

Whitney had seen it, too, and she locked eyes with Mulder, nodding, and he knew her trust in him was growing.

Chapter 5 _____

Our Lady of Sorrows Hospital
Richmond, Virginia
January 10

Dana Scully, white lab coat over her brown blouse and skirt, turned from the busy corridor into the calm of a room where her young patient, Christian Fearon, sat propped up slightly in his hospital bed, the frail, bent boy staring out the window at the whiteness of the winter morning.

"Hi, Christian," Scully said, stepping beside the bed. "You're awake early."

The pale child in the elephants-and-clowns gown gazed up at her rather blankly. "I was just thinking."

"Really? And what were you thinking?"

"About how I'm going to get out of here."

His resolve, his courage, got a smile out of her, and one that wasn't simply produced for the boy's benefit. "You know," she said, "I've been thinking about the same thing."

He nodded. His eyes weren't those of a child. *An old soul*, Mulder would say.

"So, then," Christian said, and now a faint tremor was in the young voice. "Can I get out of here soon?"

Not just resolve. Not just courage. Fear was in there, too.

Her eyes tightened. "Did something scare you?"

Again he nodded. "The way that man was . . . was *looking* at me."

She moved to the foot of his bed to check his medical chart, but found only an empty file folder. Her heart dropped to her stomach. "What man?"

The boy's eyes told her, and Scully turned to see the almost spectral figure in black that was Father Ybarra, who was out in the corridor, looking at the very charts she'd sought.

She gave her young patient a reassuring smile and a small squeeze of the arm, said, "Don't you be afraid, Christian," then strode out and up to the administrator.

Scully nodded toward the charts in the father's hands. She smiled, but her voice was sharp. "I was just looking for those."

The sad oval of his face had a way of conveying the sort of weary compassion that accompanied not hope, but hopelessness. "Good morning, Dr. Scully. I wanted to go over the charts myself . . . and, of course, the results of the new tests you ordered."

She felt herself stiffen. The administrator's presumption was beyond all bounds of professionalism.

Icily polite, she said, "That's not really your purview, Father—it's the primary physician's. Which would be me."

The line in his rumpled face might technically have been a smile, but Scully knew there was nothing friendly or supportive about it. "It is in *my* purview, Dr. Scully, to make sure all my physicians are making the best choices—for their patients, and for my hospital."

She extended a palm. "May I see the test results, please?"

He paused, then sighed and handed the charts to her. When he spoke, something genuinely regretful came in now, his concern, his tone, almost parental: "We're here to heal the sick, Dr. Scully, not to prolong the ordeal of the dying. Certainly not to add to the suffering of a child. We have moved past treatment into care—and there are other, better facilities for the boy, to serve that end."

The word *end* had a chilling sound to her, but

she could not argue with the priest's position. Not logically.

So she nodded and said, softly, "I understand," and turned away, walking off, and she could feel the father's mournful eyes on her back.

Mourning came too easy to the priest, as far as Scully was concerned. So did his willingness to allow a young boy like Christian to go all too gently into the poet's good night. This was a man of faith who surrendered readily to conventional wisdom and a hospital's bottom line.

She was walking quickly now, doing her best not to bump into anyone, doctors, nurses, nuns, patients, trying not to attract any attention though she was almost blind from the tears in her eyes, and the energy that fueled her passage was raw emotion.

Her office was a small, dark, private space where she sat down at her desk, switched on a lamp, and tried to read the charts she'd confiscated from Father Ybarra. But the tears in her eyes would not let her see. When they began to flow, she could only give in to them, breathing hard, fighting the racking sobs that wanted to take hold of her.

Fingers sought tissues from the dispenser on her desk but found it empty. She reached for her valise on the floor, got it open and fished in there, in pursuit of Kleenex, and removed several files that got in her way, and set them on her desk.

Finally she found tissues and wiped her eyes and blew her nose and generally got a grip on herself.

Breathing more regularly now, willing herself back into the professional that she was, Scully sent her eyes across the desk, looking for those charts. But Christian's files were under the FBI files that Mulder had given her. These folders were what she'd blindly removed from the valise in her search for tissues.

Now she found herself staring at the familiar FBI designation. She picked the files up, just to move them . . .

. . . and then she opened them, and began to read, to look, and to think.

Somerset Natatorium
Somerset, Virginia
January 10

The indoor swimming pool had been around for many decades, its old tile walls having seen countless children grow up, its overhead spotlights illuminating generations of swimmers in the same eerie, reflective near-darkness. Swimmers often found this restful, almost meditative, as if the old natatorium were a world unto itself, that when you swam there, you slipped into another dimension or even perhaps into the past. A handful of people were taking advantage of the afternoon "free swim" period, including Cheryl Cunningham, an attractive young computer programmer from Somerset who was sitting on the edge of the pool in a fuchsia one-piece swimsuit.

Cheryl was thirty-four, with a slim, shapely athlete's physique, her blonde hair ponytailed back, and swimming was her favorite exercise. She preferred off times like this, when she had something approaching privacy; the old, echoey indoor pool, when underpopulated, was strangely reassuring somehow, like a church you could wander into for a moment of prayer.

She slipped into the water, dunked under, then began to swim. After completing a lap, Cheryl stopped at the pool's edge to grab a kickboard there, her medical ID bracelet clunking against it before she kicked away into another lap.

Cheryl was unaware that someone was watching her, studying her, an angular-featured, muscular man who swam in parallel to her a lane over, but under water, his long dark hair streaming like seaweed. When he finally broke the surface, his bloodshot eyes continued to watch her, and she continued not to notice. Perhaps an attractive blonde like Cheryl wouldn't have been surprised to have gained the attention of a male swimmer.

Only this male swimmer stared at her with an unhealthy, red-eyed intensity. And—as another young woman had done so recently—Cheryl might have looked at this stringy-haired, angular-featured individual and thought, *Rasputin*.

But she didn't see him.

Forty-five minutes later, when Cheryl exited the Somerset Natatorium onto the facility's snow-bound parking lot—deep, plowed banks rising like fortress walls around the handful of remaining cars—she still sensed no one watching. Indeed she felt quite alone, and the solitude on this gray, over-cast afternoon suited her. Despite the cold, and her recent swim, she felt warm, nicely ensconced in her purple parka over her turtleneck sweater and jeans, gloves, snow boots, ready for anything winter had to throw at her.

She opened the rider's side of her vintage Subaru hatchback and tossed her gym bag in; then she went around and got in the car and behind the wheel, and the engine started right away, bless its heart. Behind her an old three-quarter-ton pickup, its plowing in the lot finished, turned its oversize tires toward the road, moving loudly behind her as she prepared to back out of her space. She waited for it to rumble out of her life, switched on her car radio, and soon was on the snowy country road that would take her home.

Big white flakes began to fall again. *My God, this winter*, Cheryl thought. *Enough is a frickin' nuff!* But the flurry only grew, cutting her visibility. And as her wipers batted away snow pelting her windshield, nicely in time to Gwen Stefani doing "It's My Life," Cheryl sang along—not a loud karaoke routine, just an absentminded accompaniment to her efforts to see through the ever-heavier snowfall.

Taillights glowed red up ahead.

Good, she thought. *I can attach myself to another car's rear end and make it through this stuff . . .*

Then she got a better look at the vehicle and saw that it was the old three-quarter-ton plow truck again, and nothing she wanted to get caught behind. The massive thing was plowing the right shoulder ahead and, in this snowfall, might be tricky to get around.

Cautiously she approached the big, bulky vehicle, decided there was room enough to pass on the left, and maneuvered the Subaru into the oncoming lane, speeding up a little.

But just as she began to pass the truck, the dinosaur edged over her way—maybe the driver hadn't seen her! Then after her moment of panic, the little car seemed to panic, too, hitting a slick patch, and she lost control, the Subaru slamming into the side of the plow truck.

She seemed to bounce off the truck, like a pinball, and then she was driving again but off the road, her wheels charging through a snowbank and finally coming to an abrupt stop, hitting hard drifted snow, air bag going off with a *whoosh*.

Conscious but dazed, Cheryl was barely aware of the tiny blizzard she'd stirred as it finally settled, unaware even that she was buried in her little car clear up to its windows. Breathing hard, she peered across the front seat through the passenger window, where the plow truck had stopped, and saw its driver climbing down out of the cab. He trudged through the heavy snow toward her, just a silhouette moving in, and through, the white.

Her rescuer had something over his arm, a dark folded tarp, maybe. Fairly tall, he wore a canvas coat and black jeans and snow boots, and his hair was long and black, his face impassive with an angular, Apache look. Then he was beside the passenger-side window, where he bent to look in at her.

Through the glass, Cheryl, the air bag deflated now, called, "*Hi!* Hello . . . God am I glad to see you . . . I *think* I'm okay . . ."

But, oddly, he moved from the window and . . . *what the hell?* He jumped up onto the hood of the Subaru and walked heavily across the metal, puckering, popping it. Why on earth was he *doing* that?

Then he leaped off into the snow on the driver's side, and she caught a flash of his bare hands—*no gloves in this weather?* She'd seen a large cut was on his right hand, and both his hands were blistered, very blistered . . .

Was she unconscious? Was she hallucinating?

Then his face was in her window, staring right at her with a horrible, horrifying blankness and bloodshot eyes crazily intense; dark, greasy hair dangling to his shoulders.

Rasputin! she thought.

When the window broke, she began to scream, but no one heard. And she kept screaming as she fought him, but no one saw. The snow was coming down hard now, and no one was foolish enough to be out on this road in these conditions. No one was there to hear the screams or the sound of the idling plow truck or to see its driver moving back toward his vehicle, dragging something.

A black tarp.

With something in it.

Something precisely the size and shape of Cheryl Cunningham.

Rural Virginia
January 10

Fox Mulder sat up in bed, bare-chested.

Next to him, in her mauve silk pajamas, Dana Scully faced away; but he knew somehow that her eyes were open. He had noticed, when she got home from the hospital, that an emotional day had come along with her. Still, he knew her well enough not to push. To let her process it.

Then evening had turned into night, and here in the darkness of their bedroom, she had clearly not processed it. He couldn't stand it. He had to say something. To try to help.

He said, gently, "I can feel you thinking."

Her back still to him, she said, "I'm sorry. I can't sleep."

"I might have a little something for that."

She turned to smirk at him, her hair nicely mussed, her smirk rather mussed, too. "Only a little something?"

His hand found her hair and smoothed it. "What's the problem?"

"Nothing. No problem."

"Scully."

She sighed. "I have a patient, a young boy with a rare brain disease. And he's very, very sick."

His eyes tightened. "You've been carrying this around awhile, haven't you? Why didn't you tell me this before?"

She shook her head slowly. "I thought I was on top of it. I thought there was . . . something I could do."

"And there isn't?"

She leaned on an elbow. "There are some radical treatments, yes . . . but no one seems to even want to talk about them. Even the experts say there's nothing to do."

"Nothing?"

"Nothing but let him die. And somehow that doesn't seem like an acceptable option."

He smiled a little. "No."

"So . . ." She shrugged with one shoulder. "I'm lying here, cursing God for all His cruelties."

"Yeah? And you think *God's* losing any sleep?"

Scully was looking past Mulder, into the darkness. "Why bring a child into this world just to make him suffer? I don't know what it is, but I feel such a . . . such a connection to this boy. He's got such a precious, giving spirit."

Mulder nodded. "How old is he?"

"Six. Almost seven."

He saw the pain in her lovely face and he knew why it was there. Why it really was there. Should he say?

"Mulder?"

"What?"

"You think it's because of William."

Their son, William. During a particularly dangerous, tense time for Scully—when she and Mulder had been forced apart—their child had been given up for adoption. However the couple might regret that, there was no going back.

Very gently, Mulder said, "I think our son left us both with an emptiness that can't be filled."

She shook her head. "Mulder, I've dealt with sick kids before. I've always been able to separate my feelings from whatever these young patients faced.

I don't know why I can't *now* . . . in *this* case . . ."
She sighed and turned away from him again and
curled nearly into a fetal position. ". . . when there's
nothing more to *do* . . ."

"Tell you what," he said, and touched her shoulder. "You go to sleep and I'll take over."

"Take over?"

"Let *me* curse God awhile."

She turned her head and smiled, such a lovely,
loving smile, and he kissed her cheek.

"Thank you," she said.

He kissed her again. On the mouth this time.

But she said, "Ow! Scratchy beard . . ."

Then she closed her eyes. He studied her, wondering if he'd been alone in thinking that kiss (scratchy
or not) might turn into something; but she seemed
finally to have fallen asleep, so he assumed a posture of slumber himself, and was almost out when
she said, as just a mumbled afterthought: "Oh,
there *was* something . . ."

"Something?"

"Something weird in the toxicology report on
that severed arm."

He was alert again, on his elbow. "What?"

"I looked at the FBI evidence reports again. In
the tissue, there were traces of a drug commonly
given to patients being treated with radiation. And
also traces of a drug called acepromazine."

"And *why's* that weird?"

"Because acepromazine's an animal tranquilizer."

Scully's voice indicated she was almost asleep, but Mulder was sitting up. "Now *I* can't sleep."

He got up and out of bed and left the bedroom.

Scully called after him: "Mulder . . . ?"

He was in the bathroom, splashing water on his face from the sink when he saw Scully in the mirror behind him, tying up her robe.

"Mulder . . . what are you doing?"

"Why is there animal tranquilizer in a tissue sample from a man's severed arm?"

She shrugged, rolled her eyes. "Possibly the doctor involved isn't licensed to practice, and maybe was able to obtain it through a vet."

"He said he heard barking dogs."

"Who did?"

"Father Joe."

Mulder opened the medicine cabinet, took out his safety razor and a can of shaving cream. Closing the cabinet, he saw Scully in the mirror again, and she was frowning in surprise.

She said again, "Mulder—what are you *doing*?"

He filled a palm with shaving cream and began applying the stuff to his bearded face. "Is it a tranquilizer you'd give a dog?"

But she didn't answer him, instead saying, "This Father Joe character, Mulder, he's a phony. He pulls these so-called visions out of thin air, and now he's got you straining to connect them. That's a standard carny trick, Mulder—next thing to a cold reading."

"When I see someone cry tears of blood in the snow," he said, putting on more shaving cream, "at a crime scene they recognize, without ever having visited it . . . I've got to go out on a limb and say maybe it's *not* a carny trick. You know what I mean?"

She cocked her head, eyes narrowed. "Tears of blood?"

"Tears of blood. How do you fake *that*?"

She shrugged. "I don't know how to fake that, Mulder. I don't know that it's not indicative of a medical condition, or the result of a life of depravity and dissolution . . . both reasonable routes to go down, considering. But I do know that there are limits to which obsession can affect the outcome of the inevitable."

He was in no mood to hear this. He began to shave.

Gently, she said, "It's what you were just telling me."

He'd as much as told Scully she was trying to save this sick boy to somehow reclaim William; and now she was telling Mulder he was trying to save a missing FBI agent to "find" his sister.

He could have gotten mad. He could have said, *Bullshit.*

But instead he said only, "This isn't about obsession."

In the mirror, Scully looked exhausted; she seemed to be trying to choose between finding something else to say and resigning herself to saying nothing else at all.

He paused in his shaving to turn and look at her not in the mirror but directly. "My sister is dead. This agent is *alive*."

But Scully shook her head. "I don't think she is alive, Mulder. And I don't think there's a thing we can do about it."

He turned back to the mirror and stared at her there. "I think you're wrong."

She sighed, shook her head; she seemed too tired to fight about it. She wheeled and left the bathroom, leaving Mulder stuck with just his own reflection as his beard slowly gave way to tender flesh.

Scully crawled into the bed and felt very alone, lying there quietly frustrated, knowing she had caused all this by talking Mulder into getting involved in the first place. She was wondering if she would ever get to sleep when, as if in answer to that question, her cell phone rang.

Sitting up, she frowned, trying to remember where she'd left the damn thing. Then she got up out of bed and followed the trill to the top of her dresser.

"Hello," she said tentatively. Few people had this number . . .

"Dr. Scully?" came a male voice she didn't recognize.

"Yes?" Her heart raced—was this bad news from the hospital, about Christian?

"I need to patch you through, Dr. Scully. I have Dakota Whitney calling for you . . ."

Then a connection was made and Scully could hear the sound of travel in the background, and quickly realized Whitney was no doubt calling from an FBI Expedition on yet another country road.

"I'm sorry to call you at this hour, Dr. Scully," Whitney said. Her voice jiggled a little from a fairly rough ride. "I'm trying to reach Fox Mulder."

From the doorway, Mulder, bare-chested, wiping shaving cream from his now smooth face, asked, "Who is it?"

Scully said to Whitney, "Has there been a break?"

Mulder came to where Scully stood and asked, "Did they *find* her?"

Scully heard Whitney say, "We're pursuing another lead . . ."

"From another source?" Scully asked.

"Same source. But new *news* . . ."

Scully closed her eyes in frustration as she heard, in the background, Father Joe yelling, "*Here—turn here! . . . It's here . . . it's here . . .*"

Mulder was next to her, looking like his old self, like he was about ten years old with that newly shaved mug and the earnest eyes.

"It's for you," Scully said, and handed him the phone.

Chapter 6 _____

Rural Virginia
January 11

Despite the darkness of the night—or rather of the early morning—Dana Scully, at the wheel of her Taurus, had no difficulty catching up with the FBI team. Mulder, riding next to her, had navigated—this, it seemed, was one of the same snowbound country roads he, ASAC Whitney, SA Drummy, and Father Joe had traversed the morning before.

Not that the wintry landscape past midnight didn't have its own unique beauty as well as an undeniable foreboding aspect—even before Scully and Mulder spotted the two black Expeditions parked on the shoulder, they'd seen the beams of flashlights cutting the night in ghostly streaks.

Scully drew up behind an Expedition on this otherwise long, empty stretch of moon-washed winterscape cleaved by a ribbon of asphalt. She was first to get out, bundled in her brown coat with UGG boots riding high on her jeans. Quickly she moved to Whitney, in black thermal FBI jacket, who stood in the road near an Expedition. The agent did not look happy.

Alarmed, Scully asked, "You *found* her? Was she . . . ?"

But Whitney did not immediately answer. Her ice-blue eyes had gone past Scully, who glanced back to see Mulder coming up. For just a moment, the ASAC didn't seem to recognize the clean-shaven version of the former agent. Whitney finally smiling a little in recognition at this new version of Mulder was a female moment not entirely lost on Scully.

With perhaps some irritation showing, Scully got Whitney back on point, saying, "Did you find her?"

"No," Whitney said.

As Mulder came up beside Scully, they exchanged relieved expressions. However dire the odds against the agent's survival, Scully shared with everyone else on the search team the same hope that those odds would be beaten.

"When we spoke," Scully reminded Whitney, "you said there was *news* . . . ?"

Whitney sighed and then smirked a little. "I'm

afraid the 'news' is that our favorite psychic has led us to the exact same site where he took us before." She shook her head. "I'm sorry. This was something of a false alarm. But you *are* here, so . . ."

Scully's urge was to turn around and get back in her car; but Mulder was already loping off across the snow-covered field toward where the flashlight beams were carving up the night. With a small twitch of a frown, Scully fell in behind him, and then Whitney fell in after Scully.

Those flashlight beams were trained on the ground now, half a dozen agents in their FBI jackets poring over the landscape as they kicked methodically through the heavy stuff, renewed by even more snowfall this afternoon. Leading this plodding charge was Father Joe Crissman himself, currently stopping to face a perturbed-looking Agent Drummy.

The African-American agent was breathing hard, not from exertion Scully would guess—more like annoyance, his breath pouring forth like smoke.

Actual smoke slipped from the ex-priest's lips— he was smoking a cigarette, a shambling, unshaven figure who looked more like a homeless man seeking shelter than a psychic leading an FBI search team.

Crissman, seemingly frustrated himself, was saying to Drummy, "Stay with it. You're going to *find* it—"

"That's what you keep saying," Drummy said. "Find what? *Where?*"

Crissman sucked on the cigarette. Held the smoke in his lungs. Exhaled. "You're going to find a body."

Drummy's eyes and nostrils flared. "But you keep telling us she's *alive*!"

Nodding, his shaggy hair with a nest-of-snakes life of its own, Father Joe said, "She is."

Drummy threw up his arms and shook his head and looked toward the approaching Mulder, Scully, and Whitney, his expression saying, *I give up!*

Scully couldn't blame the man. To her, Father Joe's actions put the emphasis on the first part of the word: *act*. Nothing about his behavior or his bearing seemed particularly psychic to her. She had encountered any number of individuals on the X-Files assignment who had convinced her to take the notion of psychic phenomena seriously. Father Joe did not stack up with them.

Drummy, shaking his head again, said to Whitney, "We could do this all night. Be out here till dawn. I respectfully suggest we bail."

Whitney seemed to be considering the agent's plea.

He gestured to the searchers nearby, seemingly on a snipe hunt with their flashlight beams stroking the snow. "Your people are running on empty," Drummy said.

Whitney drew in a breath and expelled it in a gray cloud. "Call it," she said to Drummy. "Let's pull the plug."

Drummy was too professional to grin at that, but Scully could tell he almost had. The formidable agent raised two fingers to his lips and sent out a shrill whistle that split the night. Then he began walking back toward the road and the waiting SUVs, the other agents falling in with him and behind him.

Whitney glanced apologetically at Scully and said, "I wouldn't blame you for being pissed off."

"It's okay."

"Really. I'm sorry for calling you out."

With that, Whitney plodded off behind the other agents.

Now Scully was alone with Mulder and Father Joe. She was about to give Mulder a look that said they, too, should bail on this effort; but Mulder's attention was on Father Joe, who was staring off into the dark, snowy distance.

Mulder asked, gently, "What do you see?"

Inwardly, Scully groaned.

Father Joe shook his head. Closed his eyes.

Really, she thought, *this is the* worst *psychic act I've ever seen . . .*

"I see a face," the ex-priest said, eyes still shut. "I see . . . eyes. Staring out."

Faint excitement edged Mulder's voice. "Who? Who is it?"

Crissman shook his head; his eyes remained closed. "It's . . . unclear. It's like I were looking through . . . like through dirty glass."

Scully gaped at Mulder. Surely he wasn't *buying* this?

"It's out there," the priest said. He moved his head as if trying to help his vision; but unless he could see through his eyelids, he wasn't seeing anything. "I *know* it."

Then the priest's eyes popped open.

Scully almost jumped a little, then thought, *Cheap effect*, and Father Joe began to walk, half in-a-trance, half dog-picked-up-a-scent. Underdressed for the chill in the tweed jacket and twill trousers, he staggered and yet moved with purpose, apparently toward a distant rock outcropping.

Mulder just watched him go, for a few moments, then mumbled, "What does he mean . . . ? 'Through dirty glass'?"

Then he went after the priest.

Scully worked to tag along. "Mulder . . . *Mulder!*"

Without looking at her, as if dazed, he said, "What?"

"Stop. *Stop!*"

But he didn't. He just kept on tromping through the snow, after the father.

Scully dogged his heels, saying, "Jesus, Mulder . . . it's one in the morning."

"Feel free to give up like everybody else."

"This is not my job anymore, Mulder . . ."

He glanced back at her. "No. It's mine. But you *are* my booking agent."

She caught up and put a gloved hand on the sleeve of his topcoat, stopping him. He turned to her, expressionless. How dearly she could love that baby face of his. And how deeply it could frustrate her . . .

"You're right," she said, her expression earnest, her eyes almost begging him. "This is *my* fault."

He smirked, half a smirk, anyway. "What do you mean, 'your fault' . . . ?"

She waved a gloved hand. "For getting you involved in this. I thought it would be a good thing for you. Get you out of that office of yours and back into the world."

He nodded, barely. "It *was* the right thing to do."

"Yes. Yes." She shook her head and gazed at him yearningly. "But not the right thing for you."

His eyes tightened a little as he stared at her; he didn't understand what she meant, and he wanted to. But she couldn't find the words.

Mulder said, "You think Father Joe is a fraud. You despise him for who he is, or anyway who he was. I get that. But, Scully—I *believe* this man."

She said it as gently as she could: "You want to believe him, Mulder."

He drew away from her, pulling his arm from her grasp.

Scully, feeling desperation rise within her, said, "This isn't about a missing FBI agent, Mulder. This is about what it's *always* been about—this is you trying to save your sister."

He gave her the blank look again. "My sister's dead."

"Yes she is. But that's never stopped you looking for her."

Mulder turned away from Scully, his eyes tracking Father Joe up ahead.

Letting all the emotion come in, Scully said, "I've been through this too many years with you. You believing you can save her. You *cannot* save her, Mulder . . . not now and not ever."

She had his attention back, all right, but she could see the resentment in his eyes.

"I'm serious, Mulder." Her tone drew a line in the snow. "I won't do this again. I won't watch you punish yourself anymore, for something you can't fix and you can't change."

He stared at her with the kind of contempt reserved only for those you love. She'd spoken with an air of finality, and they both knew that what he said next would matter—his words would be the kind that can't be taken back.

Ever.

He said, "Then don't."

Mulder's gaze moved past Scully toward the FBI agents, Whitney, Drummy, and the rest, halfway back to their vehicles. He gave a whistle as loud as Drummy's had been, and their faces turned toward the couple.

Mulder yelled, "*Hold up! . . . I need your team back!*"

The figures, no doubt a bone-tired group glad to be on the way home, stood staring back at Mulder in disbelief. Then all eyes were on the person in charge: Whitney. It would be her call.

Mulder didn't wait for the answer. He began to stride after Father Joe.

Scully, working to keep up, asked, "What are you doing?"

"Trying to ignore you."

"Because I'm right."

He rolled his eyes. "Talk about an obsession."

Finality or not, harsh words or no, they were still a couple, bickering the way only two people who'd been together forever could do.

They quickly closed the distance between themselves and Father Joe. What had appeared from far away to be a rock outcropping became in closer proximity a sheer granite face with a blue ice fall, startlingly beautiful in the midst of this stark winter landscape.

His hands outstretched, Father Joe moved slowly toward the base of the ice fall and abruptly stopped.

Then he turned to Mulder and Scully, who were

trudging up behind him. "Here it is," the priest said. "This is it . . . this is *it* . . ."

Father Joe dropped to his knees, as if to beg or perhaps pray; but then instead he started to dig in the snow.

Mulder walked up beside the kneeling man, and he, too, fell to his knees and began frantically digging through the deep white.

And Scully just stood there. Watching them. Wondering if both of them had gone mad. Wondering if the ex-priest was going through some phony melodramatics that Mulder, who after all these years should have known better, had got caught up in. Down on his knees, ready to take the Kool-Aid . . .

She could hear the FBI team returning, footsteps in the snow mingling with some grumbling as ASAC Whitney marched her team back to their psychic and the X-Files legend who was their consultant.

The two men continued digging with their gloved hands at the snow around the base of the ice fall, thrashing through the snow with a fervor that the results, so far at least, did not justify. Still, the FBI team crowded around, watching this strange, possibly pitiful sight.

Mulder glanced back at the watching crowd. "Feel free to join in," he said. "We need shovels here."

Then Mulder got to his feet and pulled Father Joe

up with him, the ex-priest looking dazed. Mulder moved him away and nodded toward the team to take their places. Like little kids hoping teacher won't insist they take a spot quiz, the agents looked to ASAC Whitney for mercy. They didn't find any.

Shovels were brought over from the SUVs, and before long the agents got to work, moving snow away from the base of the ice fall. But they, too, found more of the same: nothing. Finally they started to hit ice and could dig no farther.

Drummy, shovel in hand, approached Whitney, saying, "It's solid ice."

"No," Mulder said.

All eyes went to him. Including Scully's.

"It's dirty glass," he said.

Mulder took a flashlight from Drummy and moved in among the remaining shovelers, who were giving up. But Mulder wasn't giving up, he was if anything energized, and he sent the beam down along the revealed ice. The beam searched. So did Mulder's eyes.

Finally Mulder called, "*Here!*"

But for a moment, everyone froze, as if winter had finally had its way with them. Then the entire group thawed to rush forward and gather around where Mulder stood as he pointed the light down into the snow and where ice had been uncovered.

They all saw it. Scully saw it. And it was horrible.

A woman's head, a severed head, was encased in the ice. Her eyes were open and she stared right at them.

The dead woman was looking at them, Scully knew, just as they were looking at her: *like through dirty glass . . .*

Scully said to Drummy, "Is it her? Is that Agent Bannan?"

Drummy frowned. "It could be. Not sure. Impossible to tell . . ."

The thickness of ice indeed distorted the face of the victim.

Still, Mulder had found something; the psychic had led them to something. Yet this was no triumph, or at least Scully knew it wouldn't be to Mulder. She could see in his posture, in his face, how deflated he felt.

Glumly, Mulder said to Whitney, "You're going to need resources."

The dejection in Mulder's voice was in Agent Whitney's expression, too. This might not be Monica Bannan, true. But it might be. In fact, Scully knew, it probably was . . .

Whitney was snapping into action, however downcast she felt, yelling, "*We need equipment! Concrete saws and a backhoe. I need forensics out here ASAP . . .*"

The agents were rushing now, scurrying back to the road and the waiting vehicles. In the midst of this, Mulder stood motionless. Scully wanted to comfort him, but after the words that had been exchanged, she wasn't sure how to handle it.

When he started off toward the road and her car, she didn't fall in with him. She could tell he wanted to be alone.

That was when she realized, to her jolting discomfort, that Father Joe was standing right next to her.

His eyes were fixed upon her, unblinking.

She said nothing, her upper lip peeled back over her teeth, feeling well and truly creeped out. She experienced a shiver that had nothing to do with the cold, and then this defiler of young boys spoke to her, his words coming as if from a distant place.

"Don't give up," he told her.

He continued to stare at her, and somehow she knew this, at least, was not an act. No affectation touched the concern in those unblinking, seemingly selfless eyes.

She said nothing.

Frankly rattled, she turned and strode off and then jogged a little, to catch up with Mulder.

Twice she glanced back at the priest.

He stood there pinned against the sky, as motionless as Lot's Wife.

Still staring.

At her.

Chapter 7 _____

Rural Virginia
January 11

In that no-man's-land after midnight and before
dawn, the country road threading through snow-
packed terrain, reduced by weather to a single lane,
could be a singularly lonely stretch. Many minutes,
even an hour, might go by before a vehicle risked
passage. Two A.M. was approaching when the old
three-quarter-ton pickup truck with its oversize
tires and mounted steel plow came rumbling along
like a beast whose hide was too tough to be both-
ered by a little thing like inclement conditions.

This vehicle, which hours before had run a woman's small car off the road into the snow, made its
way up a slope; then the driver stopped it right

there—nowhere to pull off, really—and climbed from the cab. He was warm in his down-lined canvas coat and jeans and heavy boots, his hair long and dark and greasy, his features angular, a distinctive if harsh-looking man whose visage had inspired two women at two different times, linked only by the threat he had been to each, to flash on the same descriptive thought: *Rasputin.*

His name, of course, was not Rasputin, though he was indeed Russian. This cold weather was nothing to him as he moved around to the back of the truck and hauled off a bulky plastic garbage bag. Earlier he had wrapped a young woman up in a black tarp—this cargo was something else again, though even at a glance the heavy plastic bag seemed filled with unsettling shapes, as if he had spent his afternoon collecting debris from a battlefield.

As he dragged the bulky bag, his hands, despite the chill, were bare and strangely blistered, one freshly cut. Effortlessly he dragged his freight uphill, trudging through the depth of accumulation, steady in his pace. When he crested the hill, however, he pulled back immediately.

Down there, mostly in black jackets labeled FBI in bright yellow, was a search team. The group, moving in a direction that put the Russian to their backs, included former agents Fox Mulder and Dana Scully, though of course the Russian did not know this, and even if he had, their significance would have been lost on him. His reaction to this official presence, though, was almost childish in nature: He cursed in Russian, kicked at the snow, and spit a wad of phlegm into a bank by way of expressing his displeasure.

Had the FBI team encountered the Russian, their case might have come quickly to a head. But they did not. They did not see the large, threatening figure whose sharp-featured, dead-eyed face held an ugly malevolence mirroring his inner self.

Cursing again, the Russian turned and headed back to his plow truck, dragging the heavy plastic bag after him, like a singularly sinister Santa Claus. No one saw him go. No other vehicle had come along this snow-lined lane. He was alone in a bleakness washed blue by moonlight.

And when he roared off in his truck into the darkness, no one heard, except perhaps the FBI team over the hill, perceiving it as a distant, unimportant signal that life went on even after a blizzard. Life going on, though, wasn't in this instance exactly right . . .

Before long the plow truck approached a chain-link fence enclosing an oddly patched-together compound consisting of four well-worn mobile homes standing side-by-side with makeshift plywood structures tacked on, like something survivors had slapped together, post-Apocalypse. Dogs were barking indoors, stirred by the truck's arrival. The Russian jumped down from the cab, the truck motor's mountain-lion purr driving the dogs wild, and he quickly unlocked and opened a metal gate.

Somewhere within the facility, Cheryl Cunningham was still trying to define the boundaries of her limited, and terrifying, new world. Upon awakening—and she did not remember exactly when she had lost consciousness—the first thing she'd realized was that her clothing had been replaced with a white garment that she supposed was a medical gown. They had left her only her own socks.

Cheryl was in a wooden box or crate of some kind, not tiny, but not large enough to stand up in; the wood itself smelled new, plywood banged together to create this compact cell, with occasional round holes drilled to let in light and air, the way she had, as a girl, punched screwdriver holes in the aluminum foil over jars she'd kept captured fireflies in.

Her hair askew, her ears filled with the cacophony of dogs barking over one another, she was sitting on her side, leaning at one these holes, trying to get a sense of where she was, her breath heaving with the uncertainty of her position, her eyes wide with fear. Not seeing a part of the puzzle that told her anything much, she moved to another hole, through which she could see other cages, not wooden ones like hers, but rusted metal rectangular boxes with bars for walls—holding cages, and here was the source of the barking: excited dogs, snapping at nothing, eyes wild, spittle flecking.

Pit bulls.

She scooched on wood to another hole within her own cage. A wall of plastic, as you might see in a walk-in meat locker, separated this kennel from a bright room behind; through the plastic, indistinct figures moved, shadows swimming.

"*Let me out of here!*" she cried. She was already hoarse. She'd been at this awhile. "*Please!* Let me *out!*"

But the vague figures behind the sheet of plastic showed no reaction, no sign they'd heard her at all.

"I'm *cold . . . please . . .*"

A figure pushed through the plastic curtain. At first all she saw was the white hospital gown and surgical cap and gray trousers and black shoes. Then the figure, a tall, skinny man, approached, and his well-grooved, high cheekboned, gaunt face came into view, with its wide-set eyes, hooked nose, and sharp chin. He was older, in his sixties anyway, but his expression was not unkind.

For the first time, in these dire, bizarre circumstances, she felt a twinge of hope.

A younger man also in a hospital gown and cap slipped through the plastic wall and joined the gaunt doctor; they spoke to each other in a language Cheryl didn't know but thought might be Russian. They would glance her way, point at her.

But when she tried to get the attention of these two apparent medical men who were discussing her, she might have been invisible.

"*Please!* Let me *out* of here!"

Nothing.

Finally a woman emerged from behind the plastic, also in a medical gown and cap; she was carrying a blanket. The gaunt doctor took the blanket from her, with a nod and a little smile, then moved over to Cheryl's cage, and knelt as if talking to a child or one of the caged dogs (who were settling down, some).

He spoke to her, and his tone was gentle, even comforting; but his Russian was Greek to her.

"Help me, please," she said. She latched on to those caring eyes and didn't let go. "I don't want to die!"

He said something else in his kindly, incomprehensible way, and began to stuff the blanket in through a hole above her, a larger one than the little round ones she'd been spying out, this bigger aperture probably where food could be slid in.

"Please . . ."

The gaunt doctor said something meant to be reassuring, in that same language that was probably Russian. Then he gave her a country-doctor smile and got to his feet and turned and walked toward the plastic curtain, to disappear into the brightness behind it, becoming just another shadowy shape.

The man and woman in hospital gowns remained on Cheryl's side of the curtain, and approached her cage. She could hear the man unlocking something. The woman was helping.

Were they letting her go?

"I won't tell anyone," Cheryl said, her words tumbling on top of one another. "Just let me go . . . no one will ever know . . ."

But they hadn't unlocked her cage, rather some mechanism that allowed the pair to roll the entire box along, on wheels, removing her from the kennel, where the dogs had pretty much settled down now. After a few startled moments, Cheryl took advantage of the unexpected trip she was taking to see more of her surroundings, her eye at a drilled hole like a kid watching a ball game through a knothole in a fence.

But even as she watched, Cheryl pleaded: "Don't do this. Please don't do this. Let me go and I won't give you any trouble . . . I *swear* . . ."

They were pushing her through the plastic curtain now, giving her glimpses as they glided by of lab equipment, gauges and dials for measuring . . . *what?*

Then the rolling stopped.

The woman—was she another doctor, or a nurse?—swung Cheryl's box around to position it.

And though the dogs had stopped barking, some humans were doing their equivalent, a commotion in progress in here, an argument going on in that same foreign language.

Cheryl maneuvered to another spy hole and was not surprised to see the stringy-haired creep who'd kidnapped her, yelling at the gaunt doctor, clearly upset with the older man. The kinder, gentler of her captors just stood there and took it placidly as Rasputin angrily berated him.

She moved to another of the circular holes, seeking a better angle, and saw something that made her catch her breath: *a man right next to her!*

Or perhaps another captive, or maybe a patient, because he was on his back on a gurney under a sheet, only his head exposed. Cheryl had never seen the man before; but the other young woman who had been abducted, Monica Bannan, would have recognized him, because this "patient" bore the jagged, clawlike cut from her gardening tool on his right cheek.

To Cheryl, however, he seemed a potential ally. His face, though rugged, was softened by light-colored, almost feminine eyes.

And those eyes turned to her and returned her stare.

She whispered: "Please . . . let me out . . . and I'll help *you* . . ."

His eyelids, his long lashes, fluttered as he apparently tried to bring Cheryl into focus; his lips moved, too. But nothing came out.

"Get up off that thing," she whispered. "You have to get up and help me . . ."

The argument in the background continued in what she was now convinced was Russian. The older doctor was finally responding to the belligerent Rasputin in a stern, reasonable voice.

"Please," she said to the figure on the gurney, her eyes pleading as much as her voice.

He tried to get up, or anyway to Cheryl it seemed that way. And he kept trying to speak, but somehow words wouldn't come, no matter how hard he tried. She could see, in those pretty eyes, distress. Pain. Surely he, too, was a victim.

And that meant he would be no help.

She could feel tears on the way, but then he beat her to it.

The face above the white sheet contorted in sorrow and he began to cry. To weep, sending tears rolling down his cheeks dripping onto the whiteness of the sheet, dotting it with red.

The patient was shedding tears of blood.

And Cheryl Cunningham, a captive facing God knew what, discovered that after all of it—Rasputin, the struggle, the dogs, the cage, the mysterious medicos—she still had the capacity to feel a deeper strain of terror.

Our Lady of Sorrows Hospital
Richmond, Virginia
January 11

White coats sat around the conference room table intermingled with the suits and ties of hospital administrators. The atmosphere was businesslike. A discussion might have been under way to consider new policies, perhaps whether to remodel the cafeteria or expand visiting hours or maybe explore where a new charitable donation might best be spent.

But this was a discussion of an entirely different sort, which Dana Scully, just getting her lab coat on over her gray sweater and skirt, quickly gathered, coming in on the middle of a sentence.

Father Ybarra was saying, ". . . can resolve, then, in good conscience and without objection, to relocate this patient to a facility better suited for and humane to his condition?"

Taking a moment to compose herself, eyes searching out an empty seat, she said, "I'm sorry."

The skeletal Ybarra's somber face took on an uncharacteristic frown of impatience as Scully settled into a chair. "As you and I discussed, Dr. Scully, I was informing the staff and doctors of the hospital's decision on Christian Fearon."

She squinted at him, as if trying to pull him into focus. "What decision?"

Impatience turned to petulance. "To remove your patient to a hospice that will manage his palliative care . . ."

She half smiled, her incredulity at his presumptuous behavior apparent to everyone in the room, including of course Ybarra himself. "That was a discussion, Father. *Not* a decision."

The priest shrugged, then gestured to the men and women around him. "Well, it's been discussed *here* at length, and with no objection from your colleagues."

"All well and good," she said. "But *I* have an objection."

Ybarra closed his eyes. He opened them. He said, "You have, Dr. Scully, a patient with an untreatable condition. You requested outside consultation, and we sought and provided it, and that expert opinion mirrors our own. It is a sad situation, and unfortunate—no one disagrees with that."

"But he's *my* patient."

Ybarra's eyes narrowed in the long, solemn face. "Unless you've come here today with a cure for Sandhoff disease, we all respectfully request that you just let this boy go in peace."

She felt a flush of red. But she could make no reasonable objection. Logical, empirical evidence was against her.

Ybarra smiled, barely. He nodded to her. "Thank you, Dr. Scully. I'd like to wrap this up so we can get to the day's good work ahead of us. We have the final matter of a patient in intensive care. Dr. Willar's patient, I believe . . ."

As Ybarra led a discussion on this new subject, Scully sat in angry silence, the words around her a blur in her ears.

Finally she said, "There *is* a treatment."

Scully had interrupted the hospital's top administrator in midsentence, and Ybarra turned to her, stunned by her rudeness and dumbfounded by her assertion. The looks on the other faces around this table seemed to support Ybarra's diagnosis.

"Dr. Scully," Ybarra said, in a gentle tone that nonetheless had a certain edge, "this matter is resolved."

"With all due respect, Father, it's not. This disease can be treated with intercostal stem cell therapy."

A doctor across from Scully, a female colleague who'd always been supportive in the past, wore an accusatory expression. "Don't put a boy that age through hell, Dana . . ."

"Would you do it, Anna, if it were your son?"

The blonde doctor did not reply.

Ybarra said, "Well, it isn't her son. And he's not yours, either, Dr. Scully. He is just another patient . . ."

The father must have known he'd slipped, and seemed about to correct himself, but Scully beat him to it: "Is there such a thing, Father? As 'just another patient'? I hope not."

"Doctor . . ."

"This is not a decision for hospital administration. It's his doctor's decision. You all know that."

She stood, working to conceal two things: her anger and her fear. Maintaining perfect professional poise, she said, "If you want to challenge that, I'd suggest you take the matter to a higher authority."

God for example, she thought.

But Ybarra had had the same thought, making her pause at the door with his words: "I *have* taken it up with the highest authority, Dr. Scully. As should you."

She did not reply, turning and leaving. But in the corridor she felt shaken by the priest's words.

Not that it made her any less resolute.

Chapter 8 _____

J. Edgar Hoover Building
Washington, D.C.
January 11

The giant block of ice held assorted body parts, as if floating only to be caught in amber, distinct shapes despite the cloudy view, and might have been a grotesque work of surrealistic art, a fancy of Salvador Dali, perhaps, in a particularly Hieronymus Bosch–influenced mood.

But this bizarre sculpture hung suspended not in an art museum, rather in the FBI forensics lab, and was not really a sculpture at all, though it did represent the work of man in collaboration with nature, both at their harshest. The ice obelisk had been suspended from ceiling girders by block and tackle, held off the floor over a large drain by thick chains. And now a team of techs was at work on a grisly mission of recovery, painstakingly removing body parts, a head here, a forearm there, a foot, a torso, a hand, a leg from hip to knee . . .

Elsewhere in the chamber, other technicians stood or sat at various workstations, each with a separate body part already liberated from the ice. Tissue samples were being taken, as were measurements, with the appropriate tags applied. Specimens at the end of this process were being prepared for represervation in blue glycol alcohol.

In a world of lab coats or crisp FBI suits-and-ties, Fox Mulder in his sweater and jeans might have wandered in off a campus, an overage student perhaps or maybe a youthful professor. For all there was to see in this convergence of science and surrealism, Mulder was caught in the twenty-first-century limbo that was a cell phone on the other end of his, refusing to be picked up.

He paced a small area as he told the uncooperative phone, "Answer . . . *answer* . . ."

As he waited, Mulder withdrew from a pocket a small FBI-stamped snapshot of Monica Bannan, and studied it as if missing clues were eluding him there. But the pleasant image of the missing agent told him nothing. He frowned at it. Or . . . ?

He commandeered a forensic magnifying glass from a nearby workstation and took another look.

What *was* that on her wrist? Was it . . . a medical ID bracelet?

The phone kept ringing. Soon it would go to voice mail again. Scully was at the hospital, and maybe she was working, or maybe she was ignoring him.

Could she be ignoring him?

Our Lady of Sorrows Hospital
Richmond, Virginia
January 11

At her computer, Dana Scully typed in the words *stem cell therapy* and, when the countless entries came up, began highlighting those of particular interest. Her cell phone, tossed haphazardly on her desk, was ringing, and she did her best to pay it no heed, though in fact she glanced at it more than once, knowing damn well it was Mulder.

She had a case that was, to her at least, more important than that of a missing FBI agent who was surely dead. That severed head in the ice would soon be identified as Monica Bannan and this effort reclassified a murder investigation, and Mulder's interest would fade just as the FBI would renew its interest in Father Joe in a way that had little to do with the paranormal.

She hit a key and soon her printer began spewing out copies, and shortly she would have a thick stack of new information on Sandhoff disease to assimilate, opinions pro and con, treatments successful and (mostly) unsuccessful. She glanced guiltily at the insistent, trilling phone, but returned her attention to the computer screen, knowing her work was here.

Monica Bannan could not be saved.

Christian Fearon could.

Finally the phone stopped ringing, but rather than relief, Scully felt a flush of shame, knowing her partner right now was speaking to her, or anyway to her voice mail.

She did not hear him saying: "I keep leaving messages, but . . . here's what I want to tell you, Scully—that woman's head in the ice? It's not the agent. Not Monica Bannan. We don't know who it is, or why it's there, but we've pulled eleven discrete human limbs from the ice and we're not *close* to finished yet . . ."

Scully glanced at the phone, and back to her work, and again at the phone. She could not hear Mulder's words; yet she could hear him. She could hear his passion and his pain, and it hurt her.

But she had a job to do. Trying to save someone who possibly *could* be saved . . .

J. Edgar Hoover Building
Washington, D.C.
January 11

Mulder paced as he spoke to Scully's voice mail: "Every cut is a clean one—a match to that previous amputation you noted. But here's the thing, Scully—here's what you need to know . . . they've found more traces of your animal tranquilizer. Acepromazine."

A figure in a green turtleneck and black slacks was approaching—ASAC Dakota Whitney, her dark hair ponytailed back, her light blue eyes going right to Mulder as he talked and paced.

"I admit I don't know what the hell it means," Mulder told Scully's voice mail, "but I'm hoping you can make some sense out of it."

Mulder said good-bye and clicked off. He had thought Agent Whitney was headed for him, but now saw her standing with hands on hips, studying the block of ice as if it really were a work of art on display in some museum—a Grand Guignol exhibit, perhaps.

As Mulder moved in next to her, she glanced at him. "Anything?"

He shook his head. "Can't reach her. She's in the middle of a crisis where a patient's concerned. But she'll come through for us."

"I know she will."

He looked at her. "Listen, this is going to make sense. This is a break. I'm *feeling* it."

Those blue eyes widened. "You're feeling it, Father *Joe's* feeling it . . ." She laughed humorlessly. "And all I'm feeling? Is my head spinning."

"No. This is a break." He gestured to the looming ice block with its terrible contents. "You're going to solve a dozen murders here. This is a major serial you've uncovered. You should be feeling good right now. Confident."

But her eyes had narrowed and she was shaking her head. "Yet we're no closer to finding our agent."

She was right and Mulder knew it. In his enthusiasm, he'd got ahead of himself. That could happen, when he didn't have Scully around to temper his tendencies . . .

Still, he heard himself saying, "We're going to find her. I know it."

Whitney's eyebrows went up and her mouth settled into a smirk. "Well, Monica may have to stand in line."

"What?"

"I came in here looking for you, Mulder. I want you to hear Father Joe's latest vision . . ."

Within minutes they were in the conference room–cum–command center, where Father Joe was already seated at the large table with Whitney's team of agents around him like the disciples at the Last Supper.

Mulder did not join the disciples. He stood next to the seated priest, hovering over him, Mulder's face blank with atypical skepticism.

Father Joe looked up at the former agent, something sheepish in his expression. "I see a woman's face . . . *another* woman."

"Not Monica Bannan."

"She's being held. In a . . . a *box*, I think. A wooden box."

The eyes of the agents at the table were not on Father Joe now—they had, after all, already heard the priest describe this latest vision. Their eyes were instead locked upon their consultant on all things psychic, one Fox Mulder . . .

. . . who was staring at the priest in dead silence.

Finally Mulder asked, "Where is she being held?"

Father Joe sighed and shook his head in frustration, and the agents around the table were also shaking their heads, but in a different variety of frustration.

Mulder ignored that and asked, "Is she with Monica Bannan?"

Father Joe closed his eyes, apparently straining for a vision. And now the agents at the table returned their gaze to him, disciples once more.

But that didn't last long, because the priest, lids still shut, said only, "I don't know."

Mulder asked, "Is it the same men who took Monica?"

"I *think* so . . . yes, the same men."

Leaning in, Mulder pressed: "Can you *see* them?" He nodded around at the agents at the table. "Or are you just telling these people what they want to hear?"

Father Joe did not rise to this bait. He just sat there, eyes closed, and seemed to be looking into a vision, or anyway looking for a vision.

Then his eyes came open and he met Mulder's steady gaze with a simple, "No."

Mulder frowned. "No, that's *not* what you see? You were just pulling that out of your—"

"*No*, it's the same men."

Summoning his coldest stare, Mulder's eyes drilled into Father Joe with unblinking intensity, waiting to see if the priest would crack.

But Father Joe was impervious.

Mulder straightened. He took in air, let out air, and said, "I need a car, ready."

From the table, an almost scowling Agent Drummy asked, "To go *where*?"

Mulder shrugged. "I don't know yet."

Openly contemptuous, Drummy shook his head, his smile damn near a sneer as he said, "I don't *believe* this crap . . ."

The smile Mulder sent Agent Drummy was barely discernible. "That's been your problem from the start."

Drummy replaced the sneer with a scowl; but the agent said nothing, displeasure shimmering off him like heat over asphalt.

Mulder merely turned from him to Whitney and said, "A car?"

"I can get you a car," Whitney said. "Might be nice to know where it . . . where *this* . . . is going . . ."

"To tell you that," Mulder said, "I need a list of missing persons in the greater D.C. area in the last forty-eight to seventy-two hours."

Those ice-blue eyes of Whitney's were on him like Scully making a diagnosis. *Was the patient insane?* Whitney seemed to wondering.

"All right," she said. "All right."

At the table, Agent Drummy closed his eyes, but Mulder didn't figure the guy was trying to summon a vision.

Rural Virginia
January 11

Under an overcast sky, the caravan of black Expeditions was greeted by police cruisers parked along the country lane, their light bars whirling, tinting the nearby white alternately blue and red.

The lead Expedition pulled in, ASAC Whitney exiting from behind the wheel, SA Drummy on the front rider's side, and consultant Fox Mulder out the back. Other FBI agents in winter gear were climbing out of the several Expeditions pulled in behind them. As Whitney and Drummy approached the troopers, who had obviously been at their work only a short while, Mulder tramped behind the agents in their footsteps on the newly beaten path.

The little Subaru was barely visible under the new accumulation, and the state troopers at work with snow shovels had barely begun to dig it out.

As the two FBI agents conferred with the troopers, Mulder approached the mostly buried car. He was aware that today was even colder than before, everyone's breath like automotive fumes. Still, the chill hardly registered on him. He was as focused as a sniper on a target.

Whitney's teeth were chattering as she turned to Mulder to say, "Cheryl Cunningham, thirty-four. Didn't make it to work last night. No show at home, either."

Mulder, with a confidence that made the troopers instinctively step aside for him, moved to the car on the driver's side.

Drummy, arms folded, clearly shaken by the cold, said, "No blood on the air bags. Passenger-side window rolled down. Keys in the ignition."

Mulder's eyes probed inside the car.

"This is a survivable crash with a seat belt," Drummy said with a shrug. "She shakes it off, climbs out, and walks away."

As if imitating Drummy's description of Cheryl

Cunningham's probable actions, Mulder moved off from the car. He was looking around, not sure what he was looking for; he was adding things up, not sure what kind of answer he sought.

"Dark out," Drummy said, his voice louder, as if trying to break through Mulder's seeming trance, "snowing like hell. She starts off, gets tired, takes a short cut, sits down . . . and falls asleep. In this damn cold." The big African American shook his head sorrowfully. "Happens all the time."

Mulder gave Drummy the benefit of a blank gaze. "Pretty hard right turn for such a long, straight stretch of country road, isn't it?"

All those within earshot—Drummy, Whitney, troopers, FBI agents—stood there studying the scene for the next few moments, really tracking for the first time the vehicle's trajectory.

Mulder smiled that small pleasant smile that carried so much irony. "But why settle for my opinion?"

Soon, summoned from one of the Expeditions, came Father Joe, shambling along in his gray jacket and gray slacks and gray hair and beard and demeanor. The priest looked every bit as miserable as these law enforcement officers, stuck out in the cold.

Mulder crooked a finger and Father Joe came to him, at the driver's side of the partly uncovered car.

"Take her for a spin," Mulder said.

Everyone knew the car wasn't going anywhere but the priest seemed to understand.

He bent down and Mulder held the door open and the priest got in behind the wheel, pushing the now-deflated air bag away from him.

Seeing Father Joe was difficult if not impossible, from where they all stood. But all eyes were on the car anyway, as the law enforcers endured the beating wind and blowing snow, arms folded tight, waiting, waiting, and then waiting some more . . .

Drummy glanced at Mulder. "Has he fallen the hell to sleep in there or what?"

Mulder said, "They each have their own process."

"Yeah. Right."

Finally, movement.

Then Father Joe was hoisting his large frame out from behind the wheel.

He shook his shaggy head. "I'm sorry."

The priest stood there shivering, basking in the frozen silence of the law enforcers. He gestured with open arms. "I'm just not getting anything."

The priest trudged off, down the road, toward the waiting Expedition where an engine was running and warmth awaited.

"What a surprise," Drummy said.

Mulder said nothing. His eyes followed the priest, then returned to the car.

Whitney came up to him. "Ideas, Mulder? Thoughts? Impressions?" She seemed sincere, but a faint edge of sarcasm might have been buried in there, like the Subaru in the snow. She was cold, tired; he couldn't blame her.

Mulder shook his head. He lowered his eyes, feeling helpless, and then something down in the packed snow winked at him.

Whitney let out a sigh in a plume of smoky breath and said, "I think we're about finished with Father Joe."

"*About* finished maybe," Mulder said, and he knelt. His gloved fingers pried out a shiny object, uncovered by the pressure of Father Joe's footstep.

Mulder, still kneeling, looked up at Whitney and displayed a dangling piece of what at first appeared to be jewelry.

"But not *quite* finished," Mulder said.

Whitney leaned in. "What *is* that?"

"It's a medical ID bracelet," Mulder said, getting to his feet. "I noticed that Monica Bannan wore one, too."

Drummy moved in. "For what?"

Mulder just looked at Drummy. *Now* he's interested?

Whitney gave the agent a withering look of her own, then said, "Do something constructive. Get on the radio."

Drummy said, "I don't have a radio."

Whitney said nothing.

"Right."

And Drummy took off running down the road, passing Father Joe and calling to the team.

To Mulder, Whitney said, "You're thinking something."

Mulder's nod was barely perceptible.

"*What* are you thinking?"

He gave her the boyish smile; she'd earned it. "Let's pop the trunk."

The trunk of the car was still buried, but the troopers used their shovels and soon the rear of the Subaru was mostly uncovered, and Mulder, positioned on a snowbank, bent down and unlocked the trunk.

The first thing Mulder and Whitney saw was the Home Depot survival kit.

Whitney flashed half a humorless smile. "That's not going to do her much good."

Mulder was hauling out another bag—a gym bag, which he unzipped. Right on top was a one-piece Speedo swimsuit, a distinctive shade of purple.

"Or this," Mulder said.

He brought the suit to his face, and Whitney reacted as if this were an inexplicable action. Then Mulder explained with what he'd learned: "Chlorine. Suit's frozen stiff."

"That's important?"

"It means it was wet when it hit this cold." Mulder turned to a trooper. "Where's the nearest public pool?"

Somerset Natatorium
Somerset, Virginia
January 11

The old brick building seemed an unlikely place for a small fleet of black Expeditions and police cruisers to focus their sudden attention.

But if the agents in FBI-marked jackets and the state troopers in winter uniform gave the old gentleman behind the counter any cause for concern when he saw them pull up outside the facility's front window, it surely didn't show. He was rather tall, with kindly features on a long oval face, with hair as white as the weather and wire-framed glasses that, like his light tan suit, seemed immune to the swimming facility's inherent mugginess.

Mulder, Whitney, and Drummy were the first through the old double doors, with Whitney moving up to the counter to say quickly, "Hi—we're hoping you can help us . . ."

Looming behind the elderly gent was the indoor pool in its poorly lit ancient cavern, populated by a handful of swimmers whose splashes and strokes and words were magnified. Doors at right and left for men and women indicated locker rooms.

With an automatic but no less sincere smile, the old gent drawled, "Would you all like lockers?"

"No," Whitney said, more slowly. "We're with the FBI. We'd like to show you a photo, sir, if you don't mind."

He seemed mildly offended. "Why would I mind, young lady?"

Whitney had no answer for that, and Drummy produced a photo of Monica Bannan and displayed it.

"Do you know this person?" Drummy asked.

"Let me have a look." The old boy adjusted his glasses and stared at the photo. Then he shook his head. "Afraid these young people look so much the *same* . . ."

Whitney asked, "Do you keep a sign-in register?"

"Surely," he said, making three syllables out of the word. "What kind of place do you all think we're running here? I keep a sign-in sheet every day."

"Is there a chance we could see it?"

He thought about that. Then: "Well, I don't see why not. You are the law. No call for warrants or any such formalities."

Whitney smiled in relief. "Good."

The old boy pushed a clipboard on the counter toward them. "Help yourself."

"Well," Whitney said, frowning down at the clipboard, "I'd like to look at *yesterday's* sign-in sheet . . ."

"Oh! Well, I threw yesterday's away, don't you know."

Mulder had no patience for this; he could see where it was going—nowhere—and, since warrants or formalities weren't called for, he headed toward the door to the women's locker room.

"Excuse me, sir!" the old boy said. "*Sir* . . ."

Mulder was already pushing through the door, though he did hear the gent say, "Doesn't he know that's the *ladies'* side?"

Like the rest of the facility, the locker room was a relic and a rundown one at that. He paused just inside, aware that the elderly clerk had a point, and called, "Anybody in here? Hello . . . *anybody* . . . ?"

No answer.

So he went on in, and began prowling, checking the names on lockers. Many of the labels were old—faded, water-damaged. Could have been pasted on there some time in the middle of the last century. Perhaps this had once been a private club, with assigned lockers, and now was for general use and the names had never been removed.

Still, he continued to go locker to locker. He moved to the next row and, though the cold of outside had been replaced by steamy heat, he froze.

A woman at least as old as the front counter's Southern gentleman sat on a bench in her bathing suit, apparently about to remove it. She had frozen at the sight of him as he had of her. She stared at him with a blankness that threatened to turn to horror.

Holding up his palms in surrender, expecting a bloodcurdling scream any moment, Mulder instead received a smile from the old gal. A slow, impish, even sexy smile . . .

She was beginning to undo a strap when he back-pedaled and quickly was out front again.

Uncharacteristically flustered, Mulder asked the old clerk, "Do you have a bolt cutter?"

Their increasingly reluctant host sighed. "So, then, you folks aren't here for a swim?"

Chapter 9 _____

Our Lady of Sorrows Hospital
Richmond, Virginia
January 11

In the operating room, Dana Scully—in surgical cap and gown—was looking at her patient's medical charts as Christian Fearon was wheeled in on his gurney.

She moved to her patient—whose shaved head made him seem even more helpless, his frail frame swimming in the hospital gown—and gave him a warm smile. "You've got a whole bunch of people taking good care of you this morning, Christian."

The boy managed his own small smile, though it jumped a little when the gurney was locked into place.

Scully tilted her head. "Now, I don't want you to be scared."

The boy's smile seemed less forced now. "You, either."

She renewed her smile. "It's a deal."

The anesthesiologist stepped in, as Scully scrubbed up. Her face, turned away from the boy, lost its smile, and determination took over.

When she turned from the sink, Scully found her OR team already at work securing Christian's shaved head into a stereotactic clamp device. Viewing the frightful contraption, which seemed like something out of a Middle Ages torture chamber, she felt her resolve waver. Now, with all the eyes of her team upon her, she could only hope they hadn't sensed in her the doubt she'd just felt . . .

The OR nurse was frowning. "Dr. Scully . . . ?"

"We need to antiflex his head, and I need a spinal tray with a four-inch, eighteen-gauge needle. And some lidocaine in a syringe . . ."

She kept her gaze on her patient and not on those around her, not wanting any of these professionals to see her eyes and perhaps recognize the fear they held.

A syringe was handed to her, which she administered to Christian's temple, saying, "Bur drill, five-millimeter bit."

This she was handed, and she placed its nose to the child's temple.

The OR nurse turned her attention to the nearby 3D monitor, where the sight of the needle entering the boy's skull could be viewed with clinical accuracy as well as a certain distance.

By the time the procedure was complete, the afternoon had faded into early evening. Scully, her scrubs spattered with her patient's blood, sat by herself on a bench in the doctor's locker room, writing in the notebook that Christian had given her, his autographed photo on the inside cover staring up at her.

A familiar voice behind her said, "And people think *I* went underground."

She glanced toward the doorway where Mulder, in sweater and jeans, stood with hands on hips. He looked weary but alert, and she smiled automatically, but did not rise.

He came to her and sat beside her, and it was nice to have him there, but the residual tension from yesterday's melodrama did linger.

"I'm sorry, Mulder," she said, shutting the notebook. "I'm sure you've been worried. But I needed to keep my focus here."

He took in the bloodied scrubs, then met her eyes and said, "It's the boy, isn't it? Scully . . . ?"

She swallowed and nodded.

His frown told her that he could tell the weight she'd been carrying. He said, "I thought there was nothing that could be done for him . . ."

She sighed. "I'm taking a big chance on something. On a radical . . . and frankly a painful . . . new procedure."

His eyes tightened as he studied her. "Last night you said it wasn't an option, that kind of procedure."

"It wasn't, last night."

"What changed your mind?"

How could she tell him, without seeming a hypocrite and a fool? How could she say, Mulder, that ex-priest I've been calling a fraud, the one I've been criticizing you over, that priest? Well, he told me not to give up. So I didn't. Her only answer was to shrug and shake her head, and look away.

"When will you know if it's working?"

"There's a whole series of these procedures. It's going to take a while." Now she looked at him again, her expression fully confessional. "And we won't really know anything until they're all done."

Mulder nodded, and this time he was the one to look away. He was wrestling with something, she could tell; something of his own—something major.

She frowned at him in concern. "That's not what you came to talk about, is it? My patient."

"No," he admitted. He was gazing at the lockers. "Scully, there's another woman missing."

She cocked her head, as if she couldn't quite hear him. "What . . . ?"

"Another missing woman, but this one's given

us something to go on." Again his eyes met hers. "She and the missing agent swam at the same pool, Scully. We found Monica Bannan had a locker there. We think both women were stalked there. And get this—each wore a *medical* bracelet."

"Really?"

"Really. And they shared the same rare blood type: AB negative."

Interested despite herself, Scully said, "Organs—harvested for transplants."

Mulder nodded. He said nothing, staying out of her way, as she pursued the thread.

"That's how they were targeted," she said. "Donors and recipients need matched types. Somebody using that pool *knows* that . . ."

"Somebody filling orders. On the black market."

Scully was nodding. "Using that pool to find physically fit potential donors."

"Right."

"They must have access—recipients, hospitals . . ."

Now he was nodding. "*Your* world, Scully. Your knowledge of that world will save time in this thing. And, as usual, time's our enemy."

"You can start with transporters."

He was smiling, but there was something a little desperate in it. "I need you on this with me. It's starting to come together, but I need you keeping me honest . . . Look. You asked for my help, before. Now I need *yours* . . ."

But her excitement had dimmed as he made his pitch. And she shook her head, stopping him before he went any further.

"You don't need me, Mulder. And they don't need you, either, not really. You gave them your help, Mulder. Your expertise. You got them this far, broke the case for them. Let the FBI pursue it. Let them take it home."

"But, Scully, we're *so* close now . . ."

"Not we. They. And I'm asking you to leave it to them. I'm asking you to let go of it."

His smile seemed to curdle as he studied her, at first thinking she might not be serious, then knowing she was—dead serious. For a few moments, he seemed at a loss for words.

Finally he said, "It's . . . it's not that simple, Scully."

"No, it's not. It's complicated."

His face went slack. "What's that supposed to mean?"

She lifted her eyebrows. Sighed. "It means something that I must've known would happen, Mulder, finally has. Something I've been afraid to face. And that I haven't *had* to face till now."

Impatience flared in his eyes, and he said, "Just tell me *what* . . ."

"I'm a doctor," she said simply, nonconfrontationally. "Psychic pedophiles, severed heads, abducted women . . . that isn't my life now."

"I know that."

Did he?

She said, "I've made a choice in my life. I made being a doctor secondary when I went into the FBI, but I'm not in the FBI now, Mulder; that part of my life is over. This is the part of my life where I've become the doctor I trained to be. To seek the truth, yes, still to seek the truth . . . but among the living."

He was reeling inside, she could tell, but all he said was, "I'm not asking you to give it up. I would never—"

"You don't understand, Mulder. I can't do it anymore. I can't look into the darkness with you. I can't bear what it does to you . . . or me."

He stiffened, covering the hurt with defensiveness. "I'm fine with it. Looking in the dark for answers, that's where a lot of answers are, Scully. I'm actually *good* with it . . ."

"And that's what scares me."

He frowned, openly frustrated. "Where else would you have me look? If we want to find these women alive, you—"

"I'm asking you to look at *yourself*, Mulder."

"Why? I'm not the one who's changed."

Like so many arguments, this one had begun fast and degenerated faster. His petulance made Scully blanch.

"We're not FBI anymore," she said. "We're two

people who come home at night. Anyway, I come home. And when I do return to a home, our home, I don't want that darkness waiting."

Mulder gestured vaguely to the hospital around them. "This is what you do and I respect that. But we're talking about what *I* do, Scully—what I did before I even met you. It's everything I know."

"Fine. Write it down. You paid your dues, you served your time. Tell the world. Put it in a book."

Incredulous, he said, "So what are you saying? Give up?"

"You've been sitting at a computer, clipping articles from—"

"No, I'm back where I belong. Trying to save somebody from unknown evil. Back where *you* put me."

She stared at him, well aware of the ironic truth of what he'd said.

"No," she said, and looked down at her lap. "You're right. I can't tell you to quit."

The tense moment passed. Mulder seemed to ease up slightly, and she could see him looking for a way to back this up and start over.

But it was too late for that. She held his eyes with hers and said, "Here's what I *can* tell you—I won't be coming home, Mulder. I'll be staying here."

From his expression, you might have thought she'd struck him a physical blow, punched him in the belly and knocked the wind right out of him.

These were words he'd clearly never expected to hear, just as they were words Scully had never expected to utter.

Without malice, very quietly, she said, "I have my own battles to fight right now."

"Scully . . ."

"Please don't argue with me."

"Please don't do this."

She stared at him for a long time. Her expression was not without love, yet it was hard, and angry, and even wounded. To say more would be to raise, and have to answer, his unspoken question: *Not come home tonight? Or not come home ever?*

And neither could risk that right now.

So Scully just said, "I don't know what else to do."

Nothing was left to be said. She was not about to give any ground, and certainly Mulder wouldn't. Neither could abandon what they believed; they weren't made that way.

"Well," Mulder said, rising. "Good luck, then."

She nodded. "You, too."

He left quickly and she knew why: He would not want her to see the emotions that she'd already seen, just as she could not bear for him to see her face, where her hard expression was softened by welling tears.

Somerset General Hospital
Somerset, Virginia
January 11

In the morgue, a recently deceased male was receiving the classic Y incision at the expert, latex-gloved hands of a pathologist. Those hands were quickly inside the stomach cavity, working on the liver with the ease of a cook preparing a Thanksgiving turkey for the oven.

The pathologist, a tall, handsome woman of sixty in green surgical scrubs, gown, and cap, severed the liver from the viscera and withdrew it from the body, holding it in her hands and then gently placing it in a waiting medical ice chest.

The athletic-looking figure in the black-and-gray donor transport coat seemed out of place in this sterile environment, with his craggy features and stringy black hair that recently had made two women he abducted both think of the Russian madman Rasputin.

This Russian, with his own latex-gloved hands, closed the ice chest and handed the pathologist a clipboard with papers for her to sign, which she did. Then the pathologist moved on to her next deceased patient as the Russian, clipboard tucked under his arm, headed out, ice chest handle clutched in one hand. He might have been a worker lugging his lunch box.

He moved quickly down a busy corridor, talking to no one, just another professional in the medical field going about his business. He stopped at an elevator, pressed the down button, and waited.

And as he waited, he noticed several people down the hall: two uniformed police officers and a dark-haired man in suit and tie talking to a young nurse. This was not good, from the Russian's perspective, because that nurse, an attractive brunette, had helped direct him to the morgue, earlier.

And now she was pointing toward him.

Or anyway in his direction, and the Russian returned his attention to the elevator that refused to come, trying not to show his nervousness, knowing that the two cops and that young professional-looking guy were heading right his way.

And staring right at him . . .

The elevator doors slid open, and the Russian stepped on. The cops and the suit were maybe ten yards down the hall when the Russian, on an otherwise empty elevator, smiled to himself as he punched 1, feeling he was home free.

Then a hand reached in and prevented the doors from closing, instead automatically reopening to reveal the two cops and the guy in the suit, all looking right at him.

The last had dark curly hair and a young face, but his voice was confident as he said, "Can we talk with you a minute?"

"I am transporting a vital organ," the Russian said. His accent was thick but his words were precise. He only hoped the anger he felt was staying below the surface. He was unaware that his dark eyes were filled with an imposing intensity that could only work against him.

The guy in the suit smiled. "That's what I'd like to talk to you about . . ."

"I do not think you understand."

One of the cops, whose shoulder was keeping those elevator doors from closing again, said, "Please, sir—step off the elevator. Now."

The Russian heaved a sigh, unaware of the hostile arrogance in both his face and his swagger, as he finally stepped back out into the corridor.

"My name is Robert Koell," the young guy in the suit said. "I'm with the District Attorney's Office in Richmond. May I see your paperwork and license?"

Clipboard still under his arm, the Russian hesitated, then set down the ice chest. "I will reach for my wallet."

The DA's man nodded. "Go ahead."

The eyes of the cops were on the Russian like magnets on metal as the Russian got his wallet out of his back pocket. He glanced both ways down the hall, having no idea he was conveying his interest in making a break for it.

The Russian said, "I have a green card."

"Good," Koell said. "What are you transporting?"

"A human liver for transplantation."

"Your paperwork and license, please."

"You are wasting my time! You are risking a life!"

"Your paperwork and license."

The Russian handed over the clipboard and got his driver's license out of the wallet, and gave it to Koell.

"And where are you delivering this organ?"

"Cedars of Lebanon. They're expecting it. There is a patient waiting for it."

The DA's man appraised the Russian with eyes colder than the contents of the chest. "Have you ever procured or delivered an organ outside of normal or lawful channels?"

"No!"

"Ever been asked to?"

"No."

Koell gestured with the clipboard. "You're an employee of this company?"

"Yes."

"How would your employer answer those questions?"

"My employer, he is sick. He has cancer."

Koell frowned. "That's not what I asked you, Mr. Dacyshyn."

"Am I under some kind of suspicion? I am doing good work and you are wasting my time."

"Be that as it may," Koell said, and he pointed to a bank of chairs opposite the elevators, "I'd like you to sit down over here, sir."

"I don't *want* to sit down . . ."

The cop who'd spoken before spoke again: "Have a seat, sir . . ."

The Russian thought about it. He could make a stand here, that was true. These were not men who intimidated him, despite their guns. But a hospital was a bad place for it.

So he sat, ice chest on his lap.

Watching with mounting anxiety as the DA's man got out a cell phone and punched in a number on his speed dial.

Chapter 10 _____

Our Lady of Sorrows Hospital
Richmond, Virginia
January 11

When Dana Scully, her red hair damp from a shower, her mood less than cheerful, stepped into the corridor from the doctors' locker room, she almost walked straight into Margaret Fearon.

Scully, in street clothes (light blue shirt and dark blue trousers), had nothing medical in mind at the moment. She was on her way to find something edible in the cafeteria, before bunking in with the doctors on call. She was exhausted from the long operation, and the argument with Mulder hadn't exactly perked her up. She was in no mood or frame of mind to deal with her young patient's parents, but here they both stood.

They looked so young—neither yet thirty, the pretty redhead with her heart-shaped face, the tall brown-haired guy with smoldering blue eyes. Just a few years ago, these two had been all dreams of future and family; and now . . .

"Dr. Scully," Margaret Fearon said, "we're sorry to have to bother you."

Scully had the feeling the blue-collar couple had been camped out here awhile, waiting for her.

The boy's father picked up where his wife left off: "But we'd like to speak with you, if we may. About our son. About Christian."

The strained formality of that, the forced politeness, sent warning bells ringing in her brain.

Scully, her expression serious but not grave, looked from the father to the mother. "Have you been in to see your son?"

Margaret nodded. "Yes, he was sleeping. But we've . . ." She glanced at her husband with troubled eyes.

"We've changed our minds," Blair Fearon said flatly. "About going forward with this new treatment."

The parents seemed relieved now—they'd got it out. The burden of what they had to say was off them and resting squarely on the stunned Scully's shoulders.

Finally Scully said, slowly, carefully, "This is premature. We don't even know if it's working . . ."

"It's just too radical," Blair said, shaking his head. His eyes, like his wife's, were rimmed red. "We think Christian has been put through enough."

Margaret leaned forward as if to touch Scully's arm, but stopped short of that. "We know you have the best intentions, Doctor. But, after all our family's been through? We've decided—we'd like to put our faith in God now."

"Science, medicine . . ." Blair paused. ". . . it can only do so much. We need a miracle for Christian, not this . . . this *torture*."

Scully stiffened. Swallowed. "I see," she said.

The mother's eyes showed alarm. "Please! We know your intentions are the very best. But seeing our son suffer, it's just . . . it's too much, Dr. Scully. It's nothing against you, personally."

"No," Scully said.

"If . . . if you were a mother yourself, you'd understand."

After the emotional wrestling match with Mulder, this was almost too much. Scully steeled herself, fighting to maintain her composure.

Quietly she asked them, "I take it you've spoken with Father Ybarra?"

"Yes," Mr. Fearon said.

"I see."

"But the decision was ours!"

Scully nodded. Anger was creeping in, and she had to battle it back. The doubt these parents shared was reasonable, understandable, and she had to respect that.

She met the eyes of the boy's father. "What if it *did* work?" Now she met the mother's gaze. "What if later we found we'd made the wrong choice by stopping?"

Margaret cocked her head. "Are you saying you can save my son?"

"I can't promise that," Scully admitted. She had, after all, experienced her own doubts. "I just . . . I don't want to give up now."

Margaret's eyes were moist. "I know you care about Christian, very much. He thinks the world of you. We're not blind to that."

Her husband said, "But we have to do what's best for Christian, Dr. Scully."

"Then *wait*," Scully said. "Christian will be here for several days, in post-op recovery. Let's let some time pass, and not do anything rash. Then we'll talk again."

And she moved away, down the corridor, before they could say anything else.

The Compound
Rural Virginia
January 11

Back in the kennel, in her wooden box with its punched holes, Cheryl Cunningham—curled in a fetal position, blanket drawn up tight—was sleeping. She'd been sleeping for several hours and was dreaming she was somewhere better when a metallic screech jarred her awake and back to frightful reality. Her eyes popped, as another screech, with some metallic rattle in there, too, brought her to her knees and to a hole, to see what was going on.

The sounds had been the wire metal-frame doors of cages being opened, and scraping on the floor. The gaunt, tall, older man in medical gown and cap was going one by one to the caged pit bulls and letting them out. He would take them by the collar and escort them to a slightly oversize doggie door low in a wall, to push them through without any protest—this was a routine the animals were clearly used to. The woman in medical white was trailing the gaunt doctor, doing the same thing he was, letting dogs out, sending them through the doggie door into (Cheryl supposed) an enclosed outdoor run.

When the cages were empty, the job complete, the gaunt doctor moved toward her and looked in at her through the holes.

Cheryl, on her knees, hands against the rough wood of the box's walls, gave him her most beseeching look, her eyes holding his in shared humanity. "Please . . . I have a family. I have a mom and a dad, just like you. I want to see my family again. Please . . . *please*. I don't want to die. Will you please *listen* . . . ?"

The gaunt doctor gave her a kindly smile and

spoke soothingly to her. But the words were in that foreign language, Russian probably.

"I don't understand you," she said. "I can't . . . how do I . . . ?"

"Do . . . you . . . want . . . *kisses*?"

The bizarre question, in broken English, might have made her laugh if it hadn't chilled her. She could only stare at him in wide-eyed, fearful non-comprehension.

Then he slipped a hand into the pocket of his hospital gown and withdrew a cupped palm brimming with small silver objects, which he dropped through her food slot: Hershey's Kisses.

She ignored them, instead begging this seemingly gentle old man with her face, saying, "I *need* to go home—*please*. I need to go *home*!"

But he rose and ambled away, pushing through that plastic curtain into the bright room of medical machines, where earlier a sample of her blood had been taken.

"Don't *leave* me!" she called to him, through her sobs. "Don't leave me . . ."

Only he had already left.

Sex Offender Dorms
Richmond, Virginia
January 11

Her tan cashmere coat over her street clothes, Dana Scully stood at the apartment door, hesitant. She could not believe she had driven across town at night to this destination. Was she so exhausted, so emotionally ravaged, that she'd become a sleep-walker in a waking nightmare?

And yet she knocked.

It took a while for a response, but she got one, when a shocked Father Joe opened the door and stood framed there in his bathrobe and slippers, his gray hair even wilder than usual, as if he'd stuck a toe in a socket and this were the result. His gaping expression fit that post-electric-shock notion equally well.

"Now I *am* having a vision," he said. "A vision if I ever had one . . ."

She was rocking on her feet a little. Filled with trepidation, she asked tentatively, "May I speak with you?"

The ex-priest said nothing. She might have slapped him with a wet towel, the way he stared at her, openmouthed.

Then his expression settled into something recognizably human, even gentle, and he said, "Dr. Scully, I'd like nothing better."

He opened the door wider, moved sideways, and gestured. "Would you like to come in?"

Slipping past him awkwardly, Scully stepped in and almost jumped when the door shut, hard, behind her.

Again she was in the dim, gray, dingy living room. Tonight David Letterman was on the TV, getting big laughs. A blanket and pillow were on the sofa (had Father Joe being sleeping out here?), with an ashtray of spent cigarettes on the end table nearby. The fog and scent of tobacco smoke hung like a curtain. The ex-priest's world was a cold and stale one.

How many times had she and Mulder discussed the fabled banality of evil? And here she stood in a rundown flat feeling as though she'd passed through the very gates of hell.

"Make yourself comfortable," Father Joe said, gesturing to the sofa.

She shook her head. "I won't be staying long."

He moved behind her, close as her shadow, on his way to the sofa; but when he came around, he did not sit—he just stood there, staring at her unblinkingly.

"You've come by yourself?" he asked.

No, the place is surrounded, and if you make even the smallest move, so help me God, SWAT will come down on you like Bonnie and Clyde . . .

"Yes," she admitted.

Why was he staring so? To test her nerve? To gauge her timidity? Maybe just to rattle her . . .

Whatever the case, he finally sat on the sofa, saying, "Sit. Please. I insist."

She looked around for an alternate seat, but no chairs presented themselves; so finally, leaving plenty of space between them, she perched next to him on the sofa. She had to grant him that much respect—after all, she had come calling; he hadn't invited her.

"Now," he said, hands folded in his lap. "You're here to ask me something."

She nodded, and he smiled gently, apparently sensing her reluctance.

He said, "We're alone. My roommate is out. You're free to speak in confidence."

Great. Exactly what I was hoping for, to be alone with this creep . . . as if my skin weren't crawling already . . .

She sighed. "You said something to me out there . . ."

He nodded. "Yes."

". . . yesterday. Out there in the snow . . ."

"Yes. I said, 'Don't give up.'"

Now it was Scully's turn to nod. She felt strangely relieved that Father Joe had anticipated her purpose.

"I need to know," she said, "why you said that."

He shrugged. "I haven't the faintest idea. Honestly."

She stared at him.

His eyebrows rose; he smiled with something approaching chagrin. "You were hoping for another answer."

She looked away. Her thoughts had been rushing all the way over here, and they still were. She paused to compose them, then asked, "Do you know anything about me?"

His smile might have been winning, had she not known who he was. "Other than that you loathe me, my dear?"

"Had you read about me? In newspapers, or magazines? Had you looked me up on the Internet?"

"No. I don't even have a computer."

She tried again: "Do you know what I do? What I used to do, what I'm doing *now* . . . ?"

"No. But I can see you are a woman of faith."

That didn't take a psychic: the gold cross at her throat would have helped any sideshow mystic pull off a cold reading, just as she'd told Mulder.

Then Father Joe added: "But your faith is not in the same things as your *husband* . . ."

"He's not my husband."

Why had that come out so defensively? She could tell the ex-priest had picked up on that, and now his eyes fell from her face to that gold cross.

"Would you care to tell me about yourself, my dear?"

"No."

"Do you . . . do you care to offer confession?"

She gaped at him, half horrified, half disgusted. "I don't think you're in any position to . . ."

"What, to judge? Possibly not. But haven't *you* judged *me*?"

She laughed, once, mirthlessly. "Don't you deserve to be judged?"

"As a predator, you mean? A pederast? A vile abomination of God's earthly kingdom?"

"Something like that. Yes."

His smile was gentle, which creeped her out even more. "And yet, Dr. Scully, am I not God's creation, just like you?"

She got to her feet. "I don't think even God would claim you . . . not after the things you did to those boys."

She was halfway to the door when his voice, with some pulpit timbre now, stopped her: "Do you know why we live here? The men who call this ugly box of monsters our home?"

She turned toward him.

He continued: "We live here because we hate each other as we hate ourselves. For our sickening appetites."

Her upper lip curled. "That doesn't make those appetites any less sickening."

He gestured with open arms, almost as if in benediction. "So where do these appetites come from, then? These uncontrollable impulses of ours?"

"Not from God," she said.

"Not from me," Father Joe said. "I castrated myself at twenty-six."

That rocked her. This *was* hell. But it was Father Joe's hell, and she needed to get out of it. She went to the door.

"And," he said, "I didn't ask for these visions, either."

She stopped, a hand on the knob. Looked back.

He said, "Proverbs 25:2."

She frowned, offended. "What?"

" 'God's glory to conceal a thing, but the honor of kings to search out a matter.' "

"Don't you go quoting Scripture to me!"

Quietly he said, "Why did you come here?"

She said nothing, trembling. Her hand on the knob . . . but not twisting it.

He asked, "What are you afraid of, my child?"

Frowning, she said, "You said, 'Don't give up'— why? What was that *for*?"

He shrugged. Shook his head, the twisty snakes of his hair seeming to pulse.

Pissed off, she strode over to him and demanded, "Why did you *say* that?"

His eyes focused unblinkingly on her. His voice was almost a whisper: "I don't know."

"I don't *believe* you!"

"I'm not lying. I'm telling you the truth."

"They were *your* words—what did they mean?"

Again he shrugged. "I don't know why I said them."

"You looked me straight in the face . . ." She was hovering over him now, furious, her hands fists, wanting to pound on him the way a child does a parent whose strict ruling seems beyond comprehension.

And, as if her rage had set fire to his own emotions, the low-key ex-priest suddenly became distraught, eyes welling. "All . . . all I ever wanted to do was serve Him . . . all I've ever wanted was to serve my God . . ."

He bowed his head, closed his eyes, began to whisper to himself, praying apparently.

"Go ahead," Scully said. "Ask for His pity. But don't expect mine."

She was almost out the door when he began to hyperventilate. Shivering, shaking, he looked at her pitifully, and she felt he was acting again, going over the top to try to elicit the pity she had refused him.

She even said, "You can stop the act any time," but in seconds she knew—Dr. Dana Scully recognized the signs: *This was a full-blown seizure.*

Returning to the sofa, standing before the seated Father Joe, she put her hands on his shoulders.

"Look at me," she demanded, but his head hung loose as a rag doll's and his eyes were rolled back and he was swallowing his tongue.

Then she got her cell phone out, called 911, and attended to her new patient.

The Compound
Rural Virginia
January 11

As she knelt in despair within her wooden box, Cheryl Cunningham heard the sound of unlocking. Her eyes rose with the first hope she'd experienced in many hours, as she heard the gaunt doctor gently speak to her in Russian.

Then the cage door swung open as a hand reached in and put on the floor next to her a plate of warm stew, large enough that it would not have fit through the food slot where, earlier, her kindly captor had rained Hershey's Kisses upon her.

Then he shut the box's door, but before he could lock it, the medical man was distracted by other voices speaking Russian, only much, much louder. Behind the plastic curtain, dark shapes moved and harsh words were exchanged. For several moments the loud argument continued, followed by the other two medical personnel Cheryl had seen earlier, the man and the woman; both were speaking in the foreign tongue, loud, gesticulating, and the gaunt man gave them his full attention.

But as they came through that plastic butcher's curtain, Cheryl had glimpsed something startling enough to shake her, even after all she'd seen and experienced in these recent terrible hours: *A woman on a gurney was in trouble.* Cheryl hadn't seen her face, could see her only from the chest down, but that was enough of a view to see the woman's sad, sick state, the poor thing twitching, shaking, convulsing.

Cheryl of course had no way to know that at this very moment a certain defrocked, disgraced priest was experiencing an identical seizure. Nor could she understand the significance of the medical bracelet on the wrist of the afflicted woman— that the woman on the gurney was a missing FBI agent, presumed by many to be dead by now.

What Cheryl *did* know was that she had been given a chance, finally. Because when the gaunt man and his two assistants in their medical caps and gowns had pushed back through the plastic curtain, to attend their patient, the door to Cheryl's wooden cage had been left inadvertently unlocked.

As all around her, dogs barked frantically, spurred by the commotion, Cheryl seized her moment, pushing open the box's door, and then she crawled out, got to her feet; and her eyes searched for some means of escape, a door, a window, *anything* . . .

but all that presented itself was the doggie door she had seen the gaunt man and the apparent nurse pushing those pit bulls through for their evening exercise.

She knew the night would be cold, and that she had on only the hospital gown; she knew she likely would be entering a fenced-in run for the dogs. But the dogs were back in their cages, right? And she could scale any fence, and she would rather freeze out there than die here in this house of horrors, and with any luck she would get to a road or a house or at least find somewhere warm to hide.

On her hands and knees like another animal, Cheryl pushed through the doggie door and crawled into the cramped passageway—when the doggie door snapped shut behind her, utter darkness was the result—but she scrambled along, whimpering in fear, moving on sheer adrenaline, dragging herself toward the dim outline of another door at the opposite end of the tunnel.

Faster and faster she crawled. The cold air beckoned her—freedom, whatever it cost, was waiting on the other side of that small door ahead. Then her head hit the door like a battering ram and she pushed her shoulders through out into the dark and the cold, still half in the passageway.

She gulped at the frosty air.

It tasted like freedom.

Then, beyond the snowy ground, out of the

darkness, came the sound of something running, not a person, but an animal, growling, snarling, snapping, paws pounding the snow-packed earth, and before she could even see exactly what it was, Cheryl retreated into the passageway in a panic.

The doggie door slammed shut and Cheryl froze.

Then it popped open and a snarling pit bull thrust its head in, snapping at her, biting at the air around her, then another pit bull's head did the same, saliva flecking, teeth bared, eyes crazed, and she began to scream, backing up faster than she thought possible, the dogs having trouble forcing their way into the tunnel.

And when she popped back out into the kennel, and into the arms of her captors, she wasn't sure that she'd seen two pit bulls at all. But could she have seen what she *thought* she'd seen? Were her frazzled brain and the dark night and the horrific circumstances making her crazy?

Or *had* she seen a two-headed pit bull?

Chapter 11 _____

Sex Offender Dorms
Richmond, Virginia
January 11

His breath steaming in the chill, Fox Mulder climbed out of the back of the Expedition with ASAC Whitney exiting the front rider's side. While SA Drummy stepped down from behind the wheel and came around, the other two were already entering a scene washed red and blue by the whirling light bar of a pulled-up ambulance.

Moving with haste and concern toward the emergency vehicle, Mulder—Whitney a few steps behind—saw a stretcher being hauled from the apartment complex by two paramedics, with a third hauling life support alongside their patient.

Father Joe.

The priest's wild hair made him immediately identifiable, though his face was mostly obscured by an oxygen mask. From what Mulder could see, Crissman was in serious condition.

A doctor *was* on the scene, however—Dr. Dana Scully.

She was trailing along in her tan cashmere coat, part of the parade headed to the waiting ambulance. When Scully's eyes met Mulder's, her surprise at seeing him there matched his own seeing her.

Mulder went quickly to Scully and fell in beside her, their breath pluming in the cold and mingling. "What happened?"

"He had a seizure and collapsed. That's all we know for sure."

Not quite comprehending, in lockstep with Scully now, Mulder felt the tension from their locker room confrontation kick back in. "Who called *you*?"

"No one."

"Then what are you *doing* here?"

Whitney had caught up with them now, and her presence seemed to give Scully hesitation in answering. Almost under her breath, Scully muttered to Mulder, "Looking into the empty darkness."

Her manner was almost somnambulistic, and her words only confused Mulder further. He turned his attention to Father Joe, who the paramedics were loading into the ambulance.

They stopped and watched the procedure.

Mulder said to Scully, "We have to talk to Father Joe."

"I don't think that's going to happen . . . not for a while."

Whitney said to Scully, "It's important. We've got a suspect."

Quickly the ASAC brought Scully up to date on the suspect that the Richmond District Attorney's Office had interviewed about the black-market human organ trade.

Scully was frowning. "He's in custody?"

"No," Whitney said. "He was released after questioning. But I'm working on getting a warrant to search his employer's offices. *This* is the suspect . . ."

Whitney handed Scully a blown-up Xerox of a driver's license photo of one Janke Dacyshyn. Mulder watched Scully as she studied the rugged, angular face framed by long, dark, stringy hair. To her credit, Scully gave it her full attention.

Whitney said to Scully, "We've got a fairly credible witness who says our suspect swam at the same pool as the missing women. Even was seen swimming there at the same time as Cheryl Cunningham, the second victim."

Scully was still studying the photo. "Credible enough to arrest him?"

Whitney nodded. "I have agents moving in to make an arrest, yes."

Scully frowned in confusion. "Then what do you need with Father Joe?"

Irritation just below the surface, Mulder said, "To show him that picture."

A second FBI Expedition rolled in and SA Drummy was there to meet it. Mulder watched the big man talk to an agent who leaned out, then Drummy pointed toward Whitney.

"Excuse me," Whitney said, and went over to the newly arrived SUV and its several agents to see what was up.

Mulder pointed to the Xerox photo in Scully's fingers. "I'm convinced that's the man in Father Joe's visions."

She gave him a sharp look. "*Who?*"

"The suspect. Janke Dacyshyn." He tapped the photo.

She rolled her eyes. "Now *you're* wasting *their* time, Mulder."

He just looked at her. It had taken months to turn her into a partner, years to make her a believer, and here they were back to square one—him trying to get to the truth, and Scully an obstacle. How the hell had this happened?

He frowned at her. "Tell me what you're *doing here* again?"

She said nothing. Just handed the Xerox back to him.

The Expedition that Mulder arrived in rolled up

to them with Drummy at the wheel. Like a customer paying a carhop at a drive-in, a sourly smirking Drummy handed out another Xerox of a photo ID. A different one.

"Here's a vision for you," Drummy said, giving the Xerox to Mulder. "Couple of my guys brought it over."

Mulder looked at the new picture, the new face—another rugged, angularly featured man but with light-color, almost feminine eyes—with another Middle European mouthful of a name: Franz Tomczeszyn.

The former FBI agent had no way of knowing that he held in his hands photos of the two men who had attacked FBI agent Monica Bannan.

Drummy, with an edge of I-told-you-so in his voice, said, "That's our suspect's employer—an old friend of Father Joe's, we just learned."

Mulder had a sick, sinking feeling.

Scully's eyes narrowed. "You're saying Father Joe knows a guy whose business is transporting black-market body parts?"

"Allegedly transporting," Drummy said, "but yeah. Father Joe's known Franz However-you-say-it for a while. Try twenty years."

Now Scully's eyes grew large. "Twenty *years*?"

Mulder asked, "Known him how?"

Drummy savored the moment. "Seems Franz was one of Father Joe's thirty-seven very special altar boys. And three guesses who Franz is married to in the state of Massachusetts . . . ? None other than our suspect—Janke Whatever-the-hell."

Mulder said nothing. He was frankly stunned, standing in shocked disbelief as Agent Whitney leaned close and said, "We're on top of it. I have the warrant to search their offices."

He could feel Scully's eyes on him, though he sensed none of the smugness SA Drummy radiated. They had been together a long time, Mulder and Scully, and he knew she would feel for him even if this vindicated her argument.

Which it did.

Still, he could not bring himself to look at her.

Drummy pulled the Expedition sharply away, and Mulder stepped out into the lane to wave down the second FBI SUV. He wanted in on this. No matter how it played, he wanted in.

Behind him, Scully said, "Mulder . . . ?"

Finally he turned and looked at her.

"This is over," she said gently. She exuded only sadness. "Let *them* take it home."

He did not respond. She had not been smug, but the anger rose in him just the same, and he climbed into the second Expedition and slammed the door. In the rearview mirror, he saw her recede in the distance, standing there watching him go, growing ever smaller.

Medical Arts Office Building
Richmond, Virginia
January 11

The two Expeditions took the snowy streets quickly, without sirens, as it was late enough on this dark night for traffic to be light, then came to abrupt stops in front of an old three-story brick medical office building. The lights of the city winking around them, FBI agents piled out, with SA Drummy in the lead, but as Mulder climbed from the second SUV, Whitney approached him, her palm up, like a pretty traffic cop.

"Why don't you hold up, Mulder?" she said. She was blocking his way. "Let these men do their jobs."

The words stung. Like Scully, Whitney was telling him to let the FBI wind this thing up. He had no badge, he had no gun, no authority, no credibility as a consultant for that matter. Not anymore.

"Look," Whitney said. "We were all fooled on this. I wanted to believe it as bad as anyone."

"I don't know about that," Mulder said, his attention on the building the other agents had disappeared into.

"It didn't break the way we expected," she said with a shrug. "But, still—give yourself some credit. *You* broke it."

He glanced at her. "Look—I don't need the sweet talk. I'm a big boy."

"But it's true," she said with a shrug. "You led us here."

"No. Father Joe led us here—under false pretenses. That's what you believe."

"I called you in because I thought you could help me with this case. Because I valued your belief in these phenomena."

"Yeah? And now what do you think?"

"I think . . . this is a longer conversation."

Those lovely light blue eyes were trained on him in a way that conveyed an interest in him that was not entirely professional. Didn't take a psychic to figure that out.

He was flattered, but he already had one smart woman in his life who thought his obsessions were out of hand. The last thing he needed was another one.

Both Mulder and Whitney noticed the Ford van turning down a side street, but neither caught the lettering on its side: DONOR TRANSPORT SERVICES. Nor from their vantage point could they see it pull into a parking garage adjacent to the Medical Arts Building.

Within the building, SA Mosley Drummy led his team, each agent with weapon in hand, through the atrium to the stairs. At his silent command, a pair of agents broke off to take the elevator; one was conveying the compact, tubular door battering ram. Soon, on the third floor, Drummy was checking suite numbers to get a bearing on where they were headed. The little assault unit in crisp business suits made little or no noise as they stayed on the move.

The first really noticeable sound was the ding of the elevator as the two agents stepped off to rejoin the rest of the team. Within moments, Drummy was standing at a door reading DONOR TRANS-PORT SERVICES.

"*This is Special Agent Drummy with the FBI,*" he said, loud enough to be heard a floor down. "*We have a warrant to search these offices. Anyone inside, I suggest you identify yourself and unlock this door.*"

They waited.

When he felt they'd waited long enough, Drummy motioned for a man to bring up the iron battering ram. When the agent with the ram was in position to use it, Drummy again spoke: "*We are federal agents and we are armed—open the door or we will open it for you.*"

They waited.

Finally, Drummy gave the nod and the door burst open on a darkened space. As flashlight beams cut through, Drummy shouted: "*Down on the floor—down on the floor . . . Anybody here, I want down on the floor!*"

As the rest of the agents trailed into the office, the commotion covered the elevator bell dinging again, and the agents did not see their suspect, the Russian Janke Dacyshyn, in brown leather jacket and dark jeans and lugging an organ transport ice chest, emerge.

At first Dacyshyn was not aware of the FBI presence, though he frowned as he heard sounds coming from the office, and a few steps from the splintered door, he clearly heard Drummy and the agents within. Dacyshyn ventured a quick look inside, as flashlights probed the dark interior to reveal banks of refrigerators and storage units.

Then, quickly, transport chest still in his grip, Dacyshyn headed for the stairs, unseen.

In front of the building, on the sidewalk near the parked Expeditions, Mulder was pacing as Whitney continued to try to placate him. He was barely listening.

"We wouldn't be standing here," she was saying, "without your efforts. I hope you appreciate that—I assure you, *we* do. We were at a standstill and you pushed us forward, no matter the direction we took."

"Yeah," Mulder said.

"I hope to still find our agent alive, after all. I mean, that is the point of the exercise."

Mulder's eyes narrowed as a figure exited the medical building, a man in a brown leather jacket and black jeans coming quickly out of the front door, carrying something.

A chest—an *ice* chest?

The guy was moving down some steps onto the sidewalk, glancing their way furtively—a bruiser with long, dark, stringy hair and an angular face.

Whitney frowned. "Who is it?"

"The suspect," Mulder said, moving. "*Hey!*"

The guy dropped the ice chest on the sidewalk and took off running into the night, cutting from the sidewalk out into the street, alongside parked cars, with only light traffic to watch out for.

Mulder cut into the street as well, right on the guy's heels. Whitney, after a moment, took pursuit, too.

But as the foot chase over snowy cement grew from one block to two, the athletic suspect began to pull away, and Mulder, breathing hard, his brown coat flapping, was almost a third of the block back, with Whitney well behind him, though her gun was out and ready.

As he ran, Mulder hoped he didn't hit a patch of ice, the streets dusted white already, but the damp sidewalks indicated the ice might have thawed—*might*. He could easily go ass-over-teakettle at any moment, and already his gut was burning. The bruiser up ahead was in better shape than a former agent who'd been spending his days lately sitting in a home office at his computer . . .

The suspect turned a corner and disappeared, and when Mulder took that corner himself, he ran into the path of a bus whose brakes screeched as it stopped just in time to avoid squashing Mulder, who traded a startled look with its driver.

This was a more major thoroughfare but traffic remained light. Mulder could see the suspect up ahead running with the ease of a marathon man, and had lost track of Whitney, though she was coming up fast enough to pass in front of that stopped bus.

Mulder was panting but he didn't even think of stopping to rest—he wanted this bastard. Then they were on a downslope, and that made the running just a little easier. The suspect might be an athlete, but he was still stealing looks back at Mulder and seeing somebody who was not about to give up pursuit.

Pacing himself now, Mulder chased the suspect through a major intersection, though the traffic seemed mostly limited to taxis, with enough vehicles on the streets to keep Mulder from getting reckless. On the other hand, the suspect was crossing in front of cars fearlessly, while Mulder almost ran smack into a passing taxi, close enough to bounce off slightly.

The traffic grew heavier and the suspect took to running down the center line, and Mulder did the same, breathing hard but maintaining his pace, the bruiser in the brown jacket maybe three car lengths ahead, feeling safe. Then the cocky bastard jumped a chain between posts, like a hurdler, and moments later Mulder did the same, saying a silent prayer of thanks that he'd made it.

Going down a well-lighted main thoroughfare, the suspect shoved out of his way a hoodie-wearing pedestrian, crossing at the light, then leaped another chain between black metal posts, before nimbly dodging a Brinks truck making a turn. Unfazed, the suspect ran past a little park area where trees glittered with leftover blue Christmas lights. Maintaining his steady pace, Mulder could see a construction area looming ahead.

Cutting from the street, the suspect entered a covered wooden pedestrian walk as a big flatbed truck carrying a front-end loader with bucket passed by. Then Mulder was in the walk, too, his pounding feet rattling the wooden plank floor, causing the suspect to glance back at him again. Mulder smiled to himself. *Not today*, he thought. *You don't get away today . . .*

At the exit of the covered walkway, the suspect cut left and got back out in the street again, falling in behind the big truck as it went clanking along. Mulder whipped out of the boardwalk, ears filled with the sound of a commuter train passing somewhere nearby.

They were approaching a major construction area where a high-rise was going up. The suspect followed that heavy truck into an underground area where Mulder trailed his quarry down a ramp, into an excavation site where dark working conditions were lighted moment to moment by welders.

The world down here was shades of blue cut by the sparking arcing of light. Running on concrete, Mulder soon realized he was in a parking garage under construction, with equipment, scaffolding, and construction detritus all around, hanging plastic waving like lazy ghosts. The suspect was way out in front, Mulder had lost him, since the guy had followed that big truck in; then Mulder spotted the truck, which was parked now, and a white van pulled out, revealing the suspect on the run.

Mulder bore down, yelling to hardhats working here and there around him, "Hey! *Hey! Stop* him! FBI—he's a suspect! *Stop him!*"

The suspect almost got hit by the white van, veering to miss it, and headed into an area where sections were closed off with chain-link fencing, moving through an archway labeled Gate B. Mulder was back a ways, but he saw this and kept steady. He was unaware that Whitney, gun in hand, was bringing up the rear, having just come down the ramp into the excavation area.

Now the suspect was running along the chain-link fence, nimbly avoiding building rubble strewn everywhere. They seemed to have moved into a sort of makeshift junkyard, set off with red tape, labeled with a danger sign. The suspect paused in an area dominated by scaffolding and got his bearings, Mulder not in sight.

Then the suspect took off, moving past more hardhats, but Mulder wasn't far behind, moving past that scaffolding, though he did trip and almost fall on some of the littered construction crap. *Shit!*

They were deeper into the building-in-progress now, plastic draped here and there, water dripping, scaffolding everywhere. Mulder saw the suspect duck through a door and he followed, finding himself at the bottom of cement stairs in the parking garage-to-be.

"*Mulder!*"

Whitney's voice echoed behind him through the concrete chamber. He could hear the suspect's heavy footsteps above him.

"*He's climbing!*" Mulder yelled, his own voice echoing.

Up the stairs he went, and when the sound of footsteps ceased, Mulder exited from the stairwell onto the nearest floor, in the high-rise itself now, or what little there was of it, scaffolding here, building materials there, within a skeletal structure, enclosed at least.

From way down the stairwell came Whitney's voice: "*Mulder! Mulder!*"

He yelled down to her. "*I'm up here!*"

Behind draped plastic, a shadow moved, and

Mulder ran to it, pushed through the plastic into a dampish, rebar-heavy area. He could hear running footsteps and he ran, too, through the treacherous rubble- and equipment-strewn site. Before long he came to a yellow plastic curtain, and burst through and kept running toward those footsteps.

Then Mulder saw him, the suspect, running past scaffolding and through the beam of work lights, to jump over a big round duct pipe like an athletic hurdler. Mulder could do nothing so fancy; he hit the duct with a hand and hauled himself over it.

Then Mulder came into a rubble-strewn area and the bastard was gone! He put on the brakes and listened, and his ears took him to a doorless doorway in which a steel access ladder leaned against a wall.

Mulder climbed.

Then he was on the roof, or actually not on the roof, because around him loomed the light-sparkling towers that were finished high-rises, not works-in-progress like this one. This was only temporarily a roof, and would one day soon be a floor, whereas right now it was a nest of rebar waiting for concrete to be poured to make something out of it.

Construction materials, both equipment and junk, were everywhere. He stopped and listened, hearing nothing but the cold wind. The chill, however, refreshed him. His breath plumed. He felt alive.

The suspect, who'd been hiding somewhere, suddenly emerged and ran and leaped over something, Mulder couldn't tell what.

He took pursuit, and saw the suspect jump into a hole that, when Mulder got there, turned out to be an elevator shaft. His man was down there, landing hard on a wooden platform. Mulder, thinking he had the bastard finally, was just appraising the jump when the suspect leaped again, off the platform, to cling on to the steel structure of a wall of the shaft.

Screw it, Mulder thought, and jumped, hitting the platform hard, getting caught up in his coat for a moment, then scrambling over to see where the bastard had gone.

The guy was on another metal access ladder, heading down the shaft.

From somewhere below came Whitney's voice: *"Mulder!"*

Mulder yelled, *"Climbing down!"*

He had no choice: he jumped from the platform to the steel skeletal framework. He paused, catching his breath; then he made his way to the metal access ladder and started down.

ASAC Dakota Whitney, just beneath the temporary roof, pushed through yellow plastic, moving toward Mulder's voice. Then a sound caused her to whip around, and her gun tracked the fleeing figure of the suspect, running across the rubble-strewn floor.

Not having a shot, she lowered her gun and took off after him. She could hear him running, but he seemed to be above her, perhaps on a scaffolding; she entered into an area cluttered with scraps of rebar and other trash, and stood with her gun poised, looking around in this eerie half-constructed shell.

She moved around a stanchion and saw a doorless opening blocked by yellow tape. *What was this?* she thought. *A crime scene?* She leaned in and realized she'd come to the elevator shaft, then drew back a step, turning to face their suspect, who had slipped up behind her and now gave her a solid shove, pushing her into the shaft, through the yellow tape, sending Whitney windmilling.

And Fox Mulder, on a metal access ladder above, could do nothing about it but watch as she fell to her death with a scream more of surprise than terror.

Chapter 12 _____

While Fox Mulder and ASAC Whitney were pursuing their suspect, the FBI team at the medical building recovered the ice chest abandoned by Janke Dacyshyn on the sidewalk out front.

SA Drummy put on latex gloves, knelt, and carefully opened the chest. Within was a black garbage bag with something in it, something roundish, roughly the size of a bowling ball but more oblong. The bag had neither a knot nor a twist tie, and was easily gotten into, but Drummy performed this task with due diligence for the evidence it was.

Like a child looking tentatively into a Christmas gift box that might or might not contain a longed-for present, Drummy drew back the plastic and beheld the bag's contents. The agent was not easily shaken and had seen just about everything in a fifteen-year career.

But he had never before seen the severed head of FBI agent Monica Bannan.

Our Lady of Sorrows Hospital
Richmond, Virginia
January 12

Dana Scully, lab coat over her teal sweater and gray flannel trousers, was heading down the corridor to her office when she saw the familiar figure standing at the other end.

Mulder was waiting for her, his look of dejection something she knew all too well, his hands in the pockets of his brown topcoat, his expression stricken.

She wove through the doctors, nurses, patients, and nuns to join him. The couple moved to one side of the corridor and stood facing each other in a way only strangers and lovers can do.

"I know," he said, shyly apologetic. "You prefer I stay away."

She took his hand. Something softened in his face and he closed his eyes—*Mulder, Mulder* . . . He seemed to her exhausted in every way, physically, emotionally, spiritually.

"It's okay," she said in a gentle whisper. "Mulder—it's okay."

His smile was very rumpled for as tiny as it was. "I'm a little tired, I guess. And a lot confused. How it could *turn* like this . . ."

She nodded, lips pursed in a kiss of understanding.

He went on: "And how *fast* it turned. You know about Dakota Whitney?"

"I know. I heard." Her smile was warmly supportive, though she could not imagine it would help. "I tried to call . . ."

"I turned my cell off for a while." He shook his head. "I almost had him, Scully. This suspect, this Janke character."

"They filled me in." She squeezed his hand. "Don't put yourself through it again."

"How could we *lose* her?"

He hung his head. She knew how hard Mulder worked to keep his emotions behind the cool facade, but was well aware that he was suffering, largely because he was beating himself up, for what he surely viewed as failure on his part.

"Monica Bannan, dead." He sighed, shook his head again. "I thought we were winning, Scully."

For a strange moment, she processed that *we* into Mulder and Whitney, not Mulder and Scully, and she felt an absurd spike of jealousy that made her immediately ashamed.

"I know you did, Mulder," she said, and drew her hand away.

And once they were no longer touching, the reality of their lives returned in a harsh instant.

Mulder swallowed and held up a hand with rolled-up papers in it. She recognized them as the Xerox copies of the suspects' photo IDs.

"I'm here to see Father Joe," he said. "To ask him about these men."

Disappointment flooded through her. "You still want to believe him?"

He just looked at her, but the look told her she was right. She could only shake her head at the irony. To think that she had had to pull Mulder, kicking and screaming, into this affair . . .

She needed to tell him something, and she did, in a crisply businesslike way: "You should know he's been diagnosed with a terminal illness. Joseph Crissman has advanced stage bone-marrow cancer."

Mulder's eyes tightened as he processed the information. Then his expression returned to that seeming blankness that told her he remained resolute.

"I still need to talk to him," Mulder said. "I just need to be sure."

Scully could hardly deny him this final step, though her opinion of the matter was unchanged.

She said, "You need to be sure he's not just a creep, but a liar, too?"

He gave her the blank look.

"All right," she said, and held out a hand, indicating the photocopies. "Give me those. Let *me* ask him, then."

"Okay. I'd like to tag along."

She nodded, and she marched off with Mulder following.

In the oncology ward, shared with several other patients and with nurses silently scurrying, Father Joe in his hospital bed appeared frail and much older, as if the seizure Scully had witnessed had squeezed many years from him. He appeared asleep as she and Mulder approached, but when they had positioned themselves at the ex-priest's bedside, his eyes came open.

"Father Joe," Scully said softly.

But Father Joe's eyes were on Mulder, pointedly so. "Would you believe I was thinking of you?"

Mulder nodded agreeably, as if that were the most natural thing in the world for this patient to say.

"I had a vision that might interest you." He leaned on an elbow. "Of a man. Speaking a foreign language."

Mulder sneaked a glance at Scully, who shot him a dubious one in return.

Then Scully unfurled one of the rolled-up Xeroxes and showed it to the patient. "Would *this* be that man?"

Father Joe's eyes flared as he studied the rough-hewn features of Janke Dacyshyn. "*Yes!* That's the man . . ."

Was there no end to his acting?

The father was saying, "How on earth did you know?"

She said, "We think this individual abducted Monica Bannan, the FBI agent . . . as well as Cheryl Cunningham, the second woman you say you saw. Possibly he's abducted many more. And he was helped by *this* man . . ."

She showed the ex-priest the photo of the owner of Donor Transport Services, Franz Tomczeszyzn.

Father Joe studied it a long while, with a tight-eyed intensity that might have made Scully laugh if this weren't so tragic.

Finally the former priest said, "I'm sorry. I don't know who that is."

Though she felt vindicated by his obvious deception, Scully felt no sense of victory, hating to make this even worse for Mulder, who glanced at her, apparently sensing her impatience.

Mulder asked the priest, "Are you *sure*? Not just in your visions—sometime in the past, maybe . . . ?"

He shook his head. "I'm fairly certain I don't know this man."

Mulder was staring at Father Joe, obviously wishing the ex-priest had given him an honest answer.

Ready to put an end to this charade, Scully said crisply, "Well, I'm fairly certain that you do."

Father Joe turned to Scully, in seeming bewilderment.

"In fact," Scully said with a nasty little smile, "you've known him since he was a boy. An altar boy?"

Eyes still on Scully, the ex-priest's eyes widened and lowered to the Xerox she was still holding up for him.

"Oh no," Father Joe said. "Oh no . . . dear God, *no* . . ."

The ex-priest plucked the photocopy from Scully's grasp and he stared at it, agape. His eyes were welling, and he trembled under a flood of emotions. "It can't be true . . . I don't believe this is happening . . ."

"Neither does anybody else," Scully said flatly.

Through his tears, he glared at Scully, but she had no sympathy for him, no time for his lies, his goddamned lies . . .

Father Joe spoke, softly, his voice quivering but holding steady: "*He* must be my connection to the girl . . . my visions were meant to *save* her from *him* . . ."

Scully did not try to hide her contempt from the ex-priest, who turned his gaze on Mulder. "You must believe me, my son. This is God's work. God's work . . ."

Mulder was searching for words, and Scully beat him to a response, saying, "Let me ask you a question, Father. One last, simple question. Is she still alive? This girl you see, the FBI agent, Monica Bannan. Is she alive?"

The man in the bed swallowed. He seemed to sense the trap she'd set.

Come on, Father Joe, Scully thought. *It's a fifty-fifty shot . . . go for it . . .*

"I feel her," the ex-priest said. "Yes. She is still alive."

Finally the smugness came into her expression as she looked to Mulder, as if to say, *What more evidence do you need?*

Mulder merely nodded and wordlessly left the ward.

Moments later, in the corridor, she tried to catch up with him as he was walking toward the exit. "Mulder!"

He glanced back at her, but did not stop.

She worked to fall in alongside him, then asked, "Where are you going? *Mulder . . .*"

He stopped.

He turned to look at her, and his voice was soft but his tone, his words, adamant: "He may be talking about the second woman, Scully. You know as well as I that a true psychic can be imprecise about these things. That second abductee may still be *alive.*"

"Mulder . . ."

"Everybody else has given up, but if she's still alive? I'm going to find her."

She nodded. She understood. From his missing sister to the renewed sense of purpose he'd experienced of late, and everything in between, she understood it all.

He was tilting his head, appraising her, possibly wondering if she were patronizing him.

She said, "You think I don't understand, but I do."

Now he nodded. He understood, too, seemed to sense the sadness behind her words.

She said, "It's why I fell in love with you."

"And," he said, having a little trouble getting it out, "it's why we can't be together."

She wanted to reach out to him, to profess her unconditional love and tell him she'd changed her mind, but it was too late. Mulder had already turned away, leaving her alone in the busy hospital corridor.

Alone with her immeasurable sense of loss.

The Compound
Rural Virginia
January 12

The plastic curtain separating the kennel from the room where the doctors worked was askew enough for Cheryl Cunningham, crouching at a round hole within her wooden cage, to make out at least some of the activity.

The other captive she'd spied—whether he was a

patient of these doctors or some kind of guinea pig, she could not guess—lay on a gurney, all but his head covered by a blanket. The man whose rugged features were softened by light-colored, feminine eyes was obviously a very sick man, his pallor gray, his breathing weak.

The stringy-haired, scary abductor she thought of as Rasputin, in a T-shirt and black jeans, was raving out, yelling in what she'd come to accept was Russian at the gaunt, older doctor in a medical gown. What Rasputin was so upset about, she could not be sure; nor could she tell what that room was exactly, where the doctors worked in what to her was a blur of medical equipment and bright lights.

They seemed to be arguing about the sick man on the gurney, Rasputin gesturing to the patient animatedly, with anger colored by other emotions, though she couldn't tell what. Concern? Fear? *Could Rasputin be afraid of anything?*

The tall, gaunt doctor, despite his normally kind manner, was standing up to Rasputin, giving as good as he got in the heated argument. The other two, the male and female assistants in white, could be glimpsed on the periphery, giving their full rapt attention to this clash.

That was when Cheryl Cunningham saw something that convinced her she was either mad or in hell.

Rasputin, as he argued, lifted the blanket from

the man on the gurney to gesture at the body beneath, to make a point, *but what was revealed did not seem to be a man's body at all!*

Then the blanket dropped to again cover all but the head of the patient on the gurney, and Cheryl wondered if she'd been drugged and was hallucinating—could that have been, under a gown like the one Cheryl herself wore, a female body attached to a male head?

As quickly as it had flared up, the conflict was resolved, and Rasputin hurried from the room, past the two assistants and through the plastic curtain, moving out of Cheryl's view. Then she heard the gaunt doctor give crisp orders to his assistants in Russian and they were getting quickly in motion.

Coming her way!

Cheryl recoiled as the man and woman in white strode to her wooden box and swiftly unlocked it and reached in for her.

She was screaming as they dragged her out.

Rural Virginia
January 12

Like a man walking in his sleep, Fox Mulder trudged across the snowy landscape, his boots buried with each step, as he returned to, what? The scene of the crime? Father Joe had led Mulder and the FBI across this cold white desolation twice before, to dig up body parts both times.

He was looking for something, though he had no idea what. But he was drawn back to the site where the block of ice had been culled from this frigid vista and hauled away to a forensics lab for the grisly excavation of severed limbs and partial torsos. All that remained now was a chasm in the earth demarcated by surveyor's stakes and, yes, crime scene tape.

Mulder stood staring at it like a visitor to a shrine, someone who'd lost faith and hoped to regain it here. Gloved hands in his coat pockets, breath streaming in the chill, he did a slow pirouette, searching the surrounding area. His eyes stopped on a hill that overlooked the site.

He could not have explained, rationally, why he decided to check out that hilltop, but when he climbed up there, he confirmed how all-encompassing the view was. Then, when he looked in the other direction, he saw a narrow lane close by. Perhaps it was a hunch; maybe it was that this seemed the one rural lane in this patch of rural Virginia that he and the FBI *hadn't* traversed.

Whatever the reason, rational or otherwise, Mulder found himself driving down that lane in the white Taurus. This was no small task—the road had not been plowed since the last snowfall, and he was depending on ruts left by sturdier, four-wheel-drive vehicles gone before him. Though the sun was still up—presumably at least, under the clouds—his vision was compromised by yet another round of falling snow. His wipers did their best for him, but they, like the sedan itself, were being pushed way past capacity, and Mulder would be lucky not to wind up stuck out in the middle of God knew where.

The lane passed through a wooded area and then a clearing and he was relieved to come upon a plowed and well-maintained road. He had to choose between right and left, and his gut told him nothing, so finally he turned left. With no idea where he was, he followed the road through increasing snowfall into a small country town.

The Taurus slowed as it glided over recently plowed pavement through the small, seeming ghost town, its old, low-lying buildings mostly unlit, with only the occasional vehicle sharing either side of what seemed to be the main street. He was almost through the blink-and-you'll-miss-it community when he spotted an old frame building with a broad facade whose large sign read: NUTTER'S FEED AND ANIMAL SUPPLY.

With dusk settling in, closing time must have been nigh, because a stocky man in a blue plaid shirt could be seen through the glass of the front doors, apparently locking up.

Mulder pulled in anyway, and soon was knocking at the front window until the man appeared framed there looking like a rural Don Rickles with his bald bullet head and squinty-eyed expression. He opened the door halfway.

"I'm closed," the man said. Not as mean as Rickles but not terribly friendly.

"I'm sorry to bother you."

Looking past Mulder to the parked Taurus, the feed store man said, "You plan on driving that car in this weather, son, you better get to where you're going quick."

"I only need a moment of your time."

"Well, you better come in then. Let's leave the cold where it is."

And he stepped back, leaving the door open for his last-minute customer to enter, Mulder closing it behind him. He followed the man in the blue plaid shirt and jeans through aisles of animal supplies back to an old-fashioned wooden counter with feed scales and other esoteric equipment that looked ready for *Antiques Roadshow*.

He could only follow the stocky proprietor so far, because the man got quickly back behind the counter and disappeared into an office out of Mulder's sight.

The feed store man called, "What do you need, son?"

"I was wondering if you stock an animal tranquilizer called acepromazine . . ."

"Sure." He reappeared, a stack of paperwork in hand. His squinty expression had grown skeptical. "That is, if you got a prescription for it."

"I don't."

"Then I can't sell you any."

Mulder reached for his back pocket and the proprietor, perhaps thinking a bribe was coming, viewed his late customer with equal parts suspicion and impatience, a mix his scales needn't measure.

"Hold on, son . . ."

"I'm not here to buy the stuff," Mulder said. "I'm wondering if you've ever sold the drug to *this* man."

Mulder withdrew the folded-up Xerox of Janke Dacyshyn's ID photo and held it up for the proprietor, who was just about to have a look when the phone began to ring in the office behind the counter.

"Hell," he said, fairly good-natured, going off to answer it, "I'm never gonna get out of here . . ."

Mulder stood around waiting for his host's return. He could hear the man talking but couldn't really make anything out and wasn't really trying. Idly he noticed headlights coming up in the dusk beyond the front window; a large vehicle was pulling in out front, and Mulder drifted over to check it out.

What he saw was an old three-quarter-ton pickup truck with a plow prow. The driver shut off the vehicle's engine and climbed down out of the cab: *the suspect who'd eluded him at the construction site.*

Janke Dacyshyn himself.

When Tom Gibbons, the owner of Nutter's Feed

and Animal Supply, returned from his backroom office, he found the young stranger gone, and another customer waiting, a customer he'd had before, a big fella with dark, stringy hair and a face about as a friendly as a pit bull.

"What happened to that guy?" Gibbons asked his latest customer.

"Who?"

"Guy who was just standing there!"

But the stranger was nowhere to be seen.

Janke Dacyshyn, not giving a damn, just shrugged, and put in his order.

Minutes later, after hauling several bags of supplies out to the truck, the Russian got up in the cab again and took off into a snowy dusk that would soon be night. He did not notice that a white Ford that had been parked out front of the feed store, when he arrived, was no longer there.

And shortly after the plow truck pulled away from the feed store, Mulder in the Taurus pulled out from a side street and followed, at a distance.

This time the bastard would not get away.

Chapter 13 _____

Our Lady of Sorrows Hospital
Richmond, Virginia
January 12

Lost in a longing that was almost physically pain-ful, Dana Scully walked down the corridor in a kind of trance. At the intersecting corridor, Father Ybarra passed in front of her, gave her a quick, re-proving glance but no other acknowledgment, and was gone. Two nuns seemed to float by, though they nodded and smiled, and she felt as if her real-ity had passed into a dreamlike state.

But she snapped back when she looked down at the end of the corridor where the door was open to Christian Fearon's room, and she could see Father Joe, in his hospital gown and bare feet, standing at the boy's bedside, his back to Scully as he leaned down over the child.

From a dead stop she went to a full-throttle run, the disturbing image becoming ever clearer, and this was no dream, but possibly a too real nightmare: The ex-priest was at the boy's bedside looking down at him, his hand lifted in what might have been benediction but was more likely something else, something terrible . . .

Scully, filled with murderous rage, burst into the room. "Get *away* from him! Get away *now*!"

As she came around, she was relieved to see that Father Joe was simply stroking the boy's brow, the frail child with the bandaged, shaved head smiling up at him. But nonetheless Scully grabbed the priest and yanked him away, saying, "Get out of here! Get *out* of here!"

Father Joe turned to her; now *he* appeared to be in a kind of trance, or at least was pretending as much. He began, "I was . . ."

"You piece of shit," she whispered viciously. Her upper lip curled back over her teeth. "You sick *bastard* . . ."

The ex-priest shook his head, his expression that of a victim not a victimizer. "No . . . no, you don't understand . . . I was just . . ."

"*No*," she said. "I don't want to hear anything from you."

What she wanted was to drag him bodily from

the room and beat him senseless; but a crowd out in the corridor was gathering, nurses, nuns, patients, ruling out that option.

From the bed, the boy smiled weakly. He looked like a baby bird that had fallen from its nest. "It's okay, Dr. Scully. He didn't do anything bad. He's nice. Sad . . . but nice."

His angelic voice had punctured the tension, but Scully still felt the rage welling within her, while Father Joe just stood there silent as a statue, apparently stunned by Scully's outburst.

Then, slowly, the ex-priest said, "This boy is your patient . . ."

Was it question? A statement? Scully stared at him, bewilderment trumping her anger for the moment.

She demanded, "Who *told* you that?"

"No one," he said with a tiny shrug.

"Then what the hell are you doing in this *room?*"

"I've been here . . ."

She looked at the boy. "Did this man ever visit you before, Christian?"

"No, Dr. Scully."

She wheeled back to Father Joe. "You've *never* been here. So don't—"

"I *have* been here before."

"*What?*" The simplicity, the sureness of his words were almost enough to convince her of his sincerity, but she was too mad to think of him as anything but a charlatan and a child molester.

"Here in this room," Father Joe said. His tone was strange, his eyes unblinking, as if this were just now dawning on him. "You and this boy. This all happened. It's all happened *before* . . ."

Her head swimming, Scully stood there speechless. *What the hell did he mean?* she wondered, but no more words emerged from her lips to challenge him. She was still standing there staring when two hospital security guards came in and fell in behind her like the reinforcements they were.

She gave them a glance, and the two uniformed men moved past her toward the father. She knew she should stay and talk to Christian, but was too shaken to do so right now; and she was halfway out the door when Father Joe, with a guard on his either arm, said, "You've given up, haven't you? You *gave* up."

She whirled. Stopped cold, she could only stare at the eyes of Father Joe, eyes that now burned with an intensity, a religious fervor that shook her to her soul.

"You *can't* give up," he told her sternly.

Rattled, rocked, Scully turned and went out the door as if catapulted by the ex-priest's words.

Rural Virginia
January 12

Fox Mulder—guiding the white Taurus down a cleared two-lane road through snowfall and twilight—could see the plow truck way up ahead. In his FBI days, tailing a vehicle hadn't exactly been Mulder's specialty, but he felt he was doing all right—the taillights of the truck seemed a good, safe distance ahead.

He was going faster than he cared to on this road, without chains or for that matter snow tires, and his headlights were off, while the plow truck was moving along with impressive speed for these conditions in this weather.

Still, this had been going on awhile, and Mulder was feeling confident, reaching for his cell phone as he kept his eyes on the road. He noted the big vehicle up ahead as it made a tight-radius turn with surprising ease, disappearing from view.

As he took that same tight turn, Mulder was dealing with the phone, finding the right number to speed dial, and when he came around, *there was the plow truck!* . . . sitting directly in his path, stopped in the middle of the road.

Swerving, slamming on the brakes, blurting an expletive, Mulder felt a spasm of helplessness as the Taurus promptly went out of control.

With tremendous, teeth-rattling force, the sedan

slammed sideways into the stationary truck and caromed off, hardly denting the bigger vehicle, then slid into a roadside snowbank, coming to an abrupt stop that on force of impact initiated the air bags.

As his air bag self-deflated, Mulder sat dazed behind the wheel, unconsciousness seductively inviting him to a dark place from which he knew he might not return. He was fighting that, though already half out, and did not see the plow truck moving toward him and the Taurus.

But then when the plow truck slammed into the Taurus, Mulder came awake as if an alarm clock had gone off in his ear. Groggy, he looked out the side window past the sagging deflated passenger air bag and saw Janke Dacyshyn's scowl through the windshield of the plow truck as the big vehicle's prow pressed crunchingly forward into the right side of the Taurus, shoving it even deeper into the snowbank.

Mulder had gathered enough of his wits to realize what was happening, and he tried to get out the driver's-side door, but the piled snow, getting compacted by pressure, would not allow him to force it open. Desperate, he tried the window, and, unbelievably, it began to go down! Snow piled against the window was dropping away, but Mulder's surge of relief was short-lived: The snow was dropping because the little vehicle was meeting not more snow, but air.

The Taurus was being pushed off an embankment.

From within the car, which was fast becoming a coffin, Mulder could not see the worst of it: The embankment was a steep one, dropping way down to a frozen-over creek bed. What Mulder *could* see was that plow pressing against his smaller car with steady, clear, deliberate force that finally sent the Taurus over the edge, tumbling down . . .

He was conscious while the Taurus rolled over and over, ears filled with the sounds of the violent crash, and when the little car finally hit with a sickening metallic crunch, he was knocked out by the impact, no air bag left to soften the blow.

And up above, the plow truck, its headlights cutting through the darkness that had taken over dusk, backed up and then rolled away down the lonely road, leaving the crashed vehicle where the thought of anyone finding it seemed as hopeless as its driver surviving the fall.

Our Lady of Sorrows Hospital
Richmond, Virginia
January 12

Dana Scully, still shaken by the strange exchange with Father Joe in her young patient's room, stepped into the welcoming darkness of her office and shut the door behind her, leaning on it for a moment, trying to gather herself.

Finally she went to her desk, switched on the lamp, and sat down at her computer. Tapping in a password with one hand and rubbing her eyes with the other, she sat there and quietly waited for her screen to come alive.

Absently, she reached for the stack of printouts she'd made before; the sheets were in a haphazard pile and she took time to straighten them. In the process, a paper-clipped file fell to the floor. She bent down for it and placed it neatly atop her fresh stack, and large bold print caught her eye:

RUSSIAN STEM CELL THERAPY IN TRANSPLANT PROCEDURE

Below this headline was a picture of a doctor and a dog.

She frowned, staring at the page, then leafed through the file, and stopped when she came to another photo, a startling one, again of a doctor and a dog. But this dog was special.

This dog's head had been replaced—this dog had the head of another dog grafted onto its neck.

For a moment she stared at this photo as well, aghast; but then she was out of her chair, as if rocketed, digging for her cell phone in the pocket of her lab coat. She bolted from her office, hitting a speed-dial number as she went.

As she moved down the corridor, cell phone to

her ear, she heard Mulder's voice: "*I must be busy. Leave me a message.*"

"Shit," she said. She tuned out the endless messaging instruction of a robotic female voice, then said, "Mulder! I need to talk to you. I need you to call me as soon as you get this, Mulder. Believe it or not, that FBI agent *is* alive, at least part of her is."

J. Edgar Hoover Building
Washington, D.C.
January 12

In the conference room turned provisional command post, a handful of FBI agents continued to work the case, but the hustle and bustle was past. Agent Monica Bannan was dead, and so was ASAC Dakota Whitney. The hospitalized Father Joe Crissman, with his connection to alleged organ-donor black marketeer Franz Tomczeszyn, was providing the current, more limited path of inquiry.

The landline phone that rang was answered by Special Agent in Charge Fossa herself, the dark-haired, disapproving professional woman Fox Mulder and Dana Scully had noticed on their first visit to this room, but with whom they'd never actually spoken.

Right now, however, SAC Fossa was, albeit briefly, speaking to Dana Scully. But Fossa didn't handle the call. She said to SA Drummy, seated nearby at his laptop, "It's for you."

Drummy went to the phone, identified himself, and heard a female voice saying, "Mulder's missing and I need your help. I got a call from him a minute ago and I heard him yell before the line went dead."

"Is this Dr. Scully?" As he spoke on the phone, SAC Fossa hovered, an eyebrow raised.

"Yes," Scully said impatiently. "It's Dr. Scully. Look, this is—"

"Why don't you dial it down a notch or two and tell me exactly what the problem is."

"I can't reach Mulder."

"Where is he?"

"Would I be calling, if I knew that!"

"Just a moment." Drummy looked to SAC Fossa, who'd been standing close enough to hear all that; and the woman shook her head. With a sigh, Drummy returned to the conversation. "Dr. Scully, I'm going to suggest you call the police."

"What?"

"This is not an FBI matter."

"He's out there working on *your* case!"

"He's done all the work we need from him. His consultancy is over."

"You people *asked* for him! *You* called him *in*—"

"Well, that wasn't my call."

"No, it was Whitney's. And she died when she and Mulder were chasing your suspect."

"You don't have to tell me that."

"Listen to me—I need your *help*!"

Drummy's jaw clenched; she was right—they owed this to her. But his boss, SAC Fossa, was watching him with eyes as cold as they were unforgiving.

So Drummy heard himself saying, "I'm sorry. But I can't help you."

"Then why don't you let me talk to somebody with some *balls* there who *can*!"

He hung the phone up on her . . . even though he knew damn well she was right.

But he knew just as well that the one with balls, SAC Fossa, wouldn't have given Dana Scully any more relief than Drummy had been able to.

Our Lady of Sorrows Hospital
Richmond, Virginia
January 12

In the hospital corridor where she stormed down, Dana Scully had caught a few eyes and raised a few more eyebrows as she railed at her cell phone. Still moving, she punched in a number that was no longer on her speed dial, but one she could hardly forget.

An operator's voice said, "Federal Bureau of Investigation."

"Put me through to the assistant director," she said, still on the move.

"Who shall I say is calling?"

"Former agent Dana Scully."

And the next voice she heard was Walter Skinner's.

Chapter 14 _____

Rural Virginia
January 12

Despite the darkness of early evening, Tom Gibbons, proprietor of Nutter's Feed and Animal Supply, on his way to the farmhouse where he lived, spotted a hole in a snowbank that did not seem the work of Mother Nature—not judging by the various tire gouges in the white stuff just off the gravel road. The story those fresh ruts told said a car had lost control and pushed through the bank, and Gibbons knew this countryside well enough to be aware of the drop-off on the other side.

The big bald man in the insulated vest, plaid shirt jacket, and blue jeans got out of his pickup, trudged over to the roadside, and entered the doorway made by some unfortunate car, and peered down at the creek bed below, where the unfortunate car in question turned out to be that white Ford driven by that fool from the city who'd stopped in to ask a question and promptly disappeared.

Gibbons shook his head. Hadn't he warned that character about trying to drive in these conditions?

Back in the pickup, Gibbons used his cell phone. "Jim? Yeah, this's Tom. I'm out here on 154 looking at the bottom of a guy's car hoopdy-do-dooed off the road. Probably killed the poor sumbitch."

Gibbons was unaware that the "poor sumbitch" who'd been driving that car was not only alive, but, starting several minutes before Gibbons had pulled up, was doing his best to stay that way.

Fox Mulder had awakened to find himself hanging upside down, held tight by his shoulder harness and seat belt. He began working to free himself and finally did, dropping with an awkward *whump* on the overturned car's ceiling.

With the car half buried in snow, Mulder seemed trapped in the car, but he immediately started— through the driver's-side window that he'd earlier rolled down—digging his way out.

And finally, after clawing his way to freedom with his gloved hands, emerging like a gopher from the snow, he gulped frigid air, and the first thing he saw were headlights up above of a vehicle that, unknown to Mulder, belonged to the feed store man, Tom Gibbons.

Mulder yelled, "*Hey!*"

He was on his feet now, walking across the underside of his upside-down bug of a car to reach the creek bank. Then he was looking at a climb that was going to take a while, and he yelled, "*Hey!*" again just as those headlights disappeared.

Face bloodied, Mulder stood there in the dark and the cold considering his options. He patted for his cell phone, but it must have been in the car somewhere, and he didn't feel like going back down through the snow looking for it. What else was there to do but climb that steep, snowy embankment?

He started up, finding branches sticking out of the snow to cling to, though sometimes they just snapped off, but he kept at it, picking his way back up to the road.

While Mulder climbed, the Russian in the snow-plow truck was rolling along at a good clip, its driver feeling smug about dealing with that FBI agent (for to Janke Dacyshyn, who had come upon the FBI searching the Donor Transport Services offices, that was surely who Mulder was). Making a sharp turn, the Russian guided the old three-quarter-ton pickup off the gravel road onto an intersecting, unmaintained single lane that cut through white-daubed woods.

The plow truck would have to clear the way, but that would be no problem, and the vehicle's prow began its work, pushing piles of snow off the lane into mounds on its shoulders.

And for a while the plow truck did all right, creating its own path, with snow-heavy trees on either side of the narrow lane. Then the vehicle came to a sudden, unintended stop, its oversize tires spinning as the engine roared like a wounded beast. Irritated, the Russian swung down from the cab to see what the hell the problem was . . .

What he saw turned irritation into anger: The plow had cracked, from the effort of shoving that white Ford off the road, and now had sheered off. He cursed in his native tongue, voice echoing through the surrounding trees, another wounded beast complaining to a disinterested God.

When Mulder emerged from the hole created in the snow by the Taurus, cold, exhausted, the blood on his face frozen, he stumbled to the roadside and leaned gloved hands on his knees, catching his breath. The country road stretched with an apparent emptiness in either direction that could not be confirmed because of the snow blowing across. He knew that the way he'd come from offered nothing but that little bump-in-the-road town, Christ knew how many miles back. So he headed in the other direction, hoping a car might happen along.

But as he walked, the snowfall grew heavier and the wind got uglier. Staying on the road meant Mulder had to move sideways against the wind and weather, leaving him barely able to see, and his face was starting to get frostbitten.

He had faced many dangerous situations in his years as an agent dealing with X-Files cases. He had encountered monsters human and otherwise, and he had been marked for death by government conspirators, and he had faced not only death but bizarre variations upon its fatal theme that no other human being on the planet had survived, and yet here he was, about to freeze to death on a country road in rural Virginia.

When he came to the unmaintained lane that shot off in and through the woods, Mulder had no way to know that this was where his assailant, the Russian Janke Dacyshyn, had pulled in the plow truck—all Mulder could see was the part of the road that the truck had successfully plowed before it got stuck, the vehicle well out of sight from where Mulder stood, as he surveyed the fresh snowfall on what appeared to be a recently plowed path.

Mulder did consider that the plow truck that had pushed his Taurus off the road might well have plowed this lane, but not necessarily. This country road he was walking down (up?) was major enough that someone would surely come along eventually; suffering the effects of the cold as he was, he knew he should not venture into the darkness of that lane going into those darker woods.

So he chose the relative safety of the country road and again began to walk. For some reason, he remembered one time when he and Scully had been at a crossroads—turn right or left down a major road, that had been the question.

But Mulder had instead gone straight through, onto a lesser traveled lane, and that was where they had found the answer they'd sought.

So he turned around, a frozen figure somehow walking, and started down the dark lane.

Through the darker woods.

The Compound
Rural Virginia
January 12

Bright light hit her face, startling Cheryl Cunningham awake, and the sudden illumination similarly disturbed the dogs in nearby cages, who began to bark and yap. Cheryl moved to a round hole in her wooden box and saw the male medical assistant holding the plastic curtain back for the female assistant to enter the kennel with him, letting in even more of the bright light from the room where they worked amid machines and laboratory equipment.

Cheryl shrank back as the male assistant unlocked and opened the door of the wooden cage.

The man's hands reached in, and Cheryl could see the woman readying a hypodermic needle, giving it a little test squirt, and Cheryl knew just who that needle was for . . .

"*No! Get away from me! Don't . . .*"

The male medical attendant's hands were on the sleeves of the dirty hospital gown now, clutching at her.

"*Don't touch me!* Don't you *touch* me!"

The man and woman were conversing in Russian, unconcerned by her protests, their discussion purely clinical, as the shrieking Cheryl was pulled to the mouth of the cage, where the female jabbed her with the needle.

Within seconds, Cheryl had gone both silent and limp, and the man and the woman in hospital white lifted her by either arm to haul her toward the brightness beyond the plastic curtain.

Rural Virginia
January 12

Mulder had two thoughts.

First, he thought he probably had made a mistake going down this dark wooded lane and ought to turn around and go back. Second, he wondered if he couldn't just find a nice tree to rest underneath and maybe catch a little nap. That second thought, for a while, had inspired a third: *You'll never wake up.* But that third thought had faded about ten minutes ago.

Then he saw something that made him freeze and the weather had nothing to do with it: *Up ahead, in the middle of the lane, was the plow truck.*

And now he ran. Seconds ago the notion of running would have seemed absurd, even abstract. Now he ran like a track star, pumping with adrenaline, and all the snow and cold in the world couldn't slow him.

That plow truck, no lights on, sat about a football field's length ahead of him, an ungainly silhouette in a night lit only by a partial moon obscured by clouds. With no thought for safety, he ran right up to the driver's side, without considering what trouble he might have been in had the driver been there, not a concern in his frostbitten, battered, exhausted state, the adrenaline still doing its job.

But the cab appeared empty, an opinion verified when Mulder yanked open the door. That was when Mulder began to think he should take some care, in case Janke was lurking, and took perhaps a minute going all around the stuck vehicle and even letting his eyes search nearby trees not for a possible resting place, rather for any sign of the MIA brute.

The Russian did not seem to be anywhere around, although the evidence of where he'd gone was apparent: Footsteps led off in the fresh snow into the darkness. Mulder's first impulse was to follow them.

His second and overriding impulse sent him back to the cab, where he rummaged around until he found a suitable weapon. Then, and only then, tire iron in hand, did Mulder follow the footprints into the dark.

The Compound
Rural Virginia
January 12

In the operating room, Janke Dacyshyn—dressed in a medical gown and cap—hovered over the person he cared about most in the world, Franz Tomczeszyn, who lay on a gurney under a white sheet, head exposed, under the bright light of a surgeon's lamp.

Janke leaned near the other man's right ear and whispered lovingly to him, reassuring him, telling him in Russian, "It will all be okay, Franz. We will be together. We *will* be *together.*"

Barely Franz whispered, "I am afraid . . ."

"We are not going to let you die."

The male and female medical assistants rolled in the gurney bearing the unconscious Cheryl Cunningham, still wearing her soiled hospital gown, guiding it past Janke and the supine Franz and on to the gaunt doctor, who, in surgical scrubs, was taking a temperature.

The old doctor was not taking the temperature of a patient, however: He was testing the water in a large plastic tub filled with slushy ice.

Then the gaunt doctor turned to his two assistants and gave them stern, crisp orders in Russian as they conveyed Cheryl Cunningham from the gurney to the tub of murky cold slush, stripped her soiled hospital gown from her flesh, and put her carefully down in it, making sure her head was elevated from her body so that she could breathe.

Heavily sedated though she was, Cheryl reacted at the extreme cold, sitting up; but the male and female assistant forced her back down, immersing her in the slush, but for her head, of course.

The tall, gaunt doctor, who had seemed compassionate to Cheryl, had nothing in his expression now except businesslike determination. He moved to the gurney where Franz awaited and lifted the sheet back off, revealing sutures on his patient's neck, a line of demarcation between the man's head above and the woman's body below.

Monica Bannan's body was still alive, but only technically. Her flesh was a discolored gray, the life draining out of it: The woman's body beneath the thick, dark sutures binding it to the man's head was dying.

The gaunt doctor began to snip the sutures. The procedure was about to begin. That is, it would begin as soon as the remnants of their first failed attempt were removed and discarded—the headless body of a female FBI agent.

Mulder's footfalls crunched in the untrammeled snow, lightly powdered with fresh snowfall, as he followed the Russian's path to a clearing.

He could see an odd arrangement of structures up ahead. Beyond a chain-link fence, in the jaundiced cast of dim, yellow exterior lighting courtesy of a humming generator, yawned an ungainly, cobbled-together . . . what? Building? Facility?

Mulder counted four weathered-looking mobile homes side by side with makeshift plywood structures added on, remote from civilization, but up to something . . .

Staying low, tire iron at the ready, he moved closer.

His thick surgeon's glasses magnifying his eyes grotesquely, the tall, gaunt doctor focused intensely on his work, his scalpel poised at the neck of Franz Tomczeszyn. In Russian, he asked his female assistant for a tool and she handed him tongs, the sutured artery he was working on reflected in his glasses.

Janke Dacyshyn, looking like another medical assistant in the gown and cap but really just intruding on the doctor's space, leaned in over Franz on the gurney and again whispered in urgent Russian: "You are going to live, Franz. You are going to have a fine, strong body again . . . the body you have always dreamed of . . ."

Franz weakly tried to respond, but the gaunt doctor—no sign of kindliness now—snapped at them in Russian, and the burly Janke backed off like a scolded child. As if by way of consolation, Janke sent his eyes to the tub of slush where the sedated Cheryl Cunningham was nakedly immersed, and considered the "fine, strong body" he'd been referring to.

And right now Cheryl was being prepared, the male assistant painting a collar of yellow iodine around her neck, indicating the precise spot where her head would be surgically removed.

Mulder climbed the fence, his coat and gloves protecting him from the upper layer of barbed wire, and dropped in relative silence to the snow on the inner ground outside the makeshift facility. Keeping low, he crept toward the trailers at the center of the fenced-off area. Movement behind him startled him, and he turned and saw the dark silhouette of a dog.

The animal was growling. So was another dog, apparently nearby, but Mulder saw only the one beast, and he was thinking of heading back for the fence when the creature charged at him, more a dark shape than anything real, but the vicious growling, coming at him in stereo, seemed real enough. *But where was the second dog?*

He braced himself for the attack as the animal, running low and fast, came at him full speed, leaving the ground to go for Mulder's throat, and when the dog made its leap, it passed through yellow light and Mulder saw not one but two heads on the creature, two saliva-spitting, teeth-gnashing heads on a single canine body.

In the operating room, the gaunt doctor—his magnified eyes focused intensely on the scalpel at Franz Tomczeszyn's neck—was startled by the sound of barking dogs. The barking came from outside the building but set off an immediate chain reaction of noisy animals in the adjacent kennel, and the doctor screamed orders in Russian. His two assistants came immediately to his side.

Then, to Janke Dacyshyn, he said in Russian, "You expect me to perform miracles in this madhouse! *Do* something!"

Janke moved quickly from the operating room, through the curtain and into the kennel, while the gaunt doctor went to the plastic tub where waited Cheryl Cunningham, her inert body only faintly visible in the murky slush, though the painted yellow iodine at her neck was plain to see.

The doctor touched her neck with his scalpel.

In the meantime, Janke had rushed out a door

into the cold air of the fenced-in compound, eyes searching the yellow-tinged night for the source of the commotion. The Russian, still in his medical gown and cap, could hear nothing, and saw nothing of note until finally his gaze landed on something brown and bulky over by the fence line.

The Russian moved toward the shape until finally it became the brown coat that that FBI agent had been wearing! As he grew closer, he could see that the cloth was torn, ripped, and Janke figured one of the animals had got hold of the intruder.

This assumption was borne out by the heaving shape in the snow that was a bloody, badly injured dog. The creature was literally half dead, one head panting, the other with its skull bashed in.

The Russian could make out a trail of blood leading away from the fallen creature, footsteps apparent in the snow, heading toward the facility. He retraced the intruder's path around the corner of the trailers, and they disappeared, blending into a muddy footpath.

No sign of the intruder anywhere within the fenced-in area. But Janke would find him.

And finish the job the two-headed beast had started.

Chapter 15 _____

Rural Virginia
January 12

A tow truck was winching the battered white Taurus up out of the creek bed when the black Expedition came up the country road fast and pulled into a stop behind a police cruiser, whose light bar was painting white banks red and blue, like snow cones drizzled with bright syrup. But there was nothing festive about this grim scene.

Her tan cashmere coat flapping in the flake-flecked wind, Dana Scully got quickly down from the rider's side and approached an impossibly young-looking uniformed officer.

"I'm Dana Scully," she told him, with a nod toward the vehicle being craned. "That's my car."

"Right," the officer said. "I have your name. I spoke to some bigwig at the FBI who called over from Washington."

"Walter Skinner," Scully said with another nod.

The cop was looking past Scully at the tall male figure in a dark topcoat getting out on the driver's side of the SUV.

"That's him," Scully said.

Because of the call Skinner had made earlier, Scully already knew the crashed vehicle was empty; but she asked the officer, "Any sign of the driver?"

He held up something that had been in his right gloved hand: Mulder's cell phone. Something dark reddish-black crusted the phone's earpiece.

"Found this thrown clear, stuck in a snowbank," the officer said. "Figure the driver was on his cell when the crash happened—had his window down for some reason."

Scully took the phone, and the cop had an expression that said he probably should have protested (but he didn't), and she turned and strode to meet the approaching Skinner halfway.

"Officer found this," she said, shaken. "It's got blood on it."

Assistant FBI Director Walter Skinner was a commanding figure who, at six-one, towered over the petite ex-agent. Bald, bespectacled, with a professorial mien but the build of an athlete, Skinner radiated a deceptive calmness, a professional cool, that concealed heat. This man had been much more than a boss to Scully and Mulder, and could swing into decisive action like a man half his fifty-some years.

That she was upset by the discovery of the blood-spattered cell phone was not lost on Skinner, who said, "Just calm down—stop and think."

He was right, but she couldn't do it—my God, she was hyperventilating! *Get a grip!* she told herself.

Skinner took her gently but firmly by the shoulders. "Listen, he's okay. He's got to be. Look at the scene—be an investigator again."

She swallowed and nodded and turned back to take in the wreck being pulled up with skill and care by the African-American woman at the wheel of the tow truck.

Thoughtful, Skinner ambled closer, and Scully tagged along as he said, "Mulder climbed out of there somehow, down below . . . and if he climbed *out*, he probably climbed *up* . . ."

"I'll buy that," she said, calmer now. "But where did he *go*?"

Skinner's thin lips twitched something that was neither smile nor frown, merely an acknowledgment that he had no idea what the answer to that question was.

Nor did Scully.

The Compound
Rural Virginia
January 12

At the same moment Dana Scully and Walter Skinner were wondering where the hell Fox Mulder could be, Janke Dacyshyn—following the muddy path around the conjoined mobile homes—was wondering the same thing, though the name Fox Mulder would have meant nothing to him. He had identified Mulder as an FBI agent and right now presumed the intruder had, with some weapon or other, split in half the head of (well, one head of) the now dead two-headed dog.

As he continued his search, the Russian moved by the small doggie door that concealed the answer to his question: Mulder had crawled through into a dark tunnel designed for dogs but accommodating, if tightly, the bloody, cold, exhausted former FBI agent.

Mulder crawled through the tunnel and soon emerged into what he saw was a cramped kennel where a number of one-headed dogs slumbered. Not wanting to wake them and have his presence announced, he got quietly to his feet and surveyed his surroundings.

What his attention went to immediately was the plastic curtain separating the kennel from an adjacent, brightly lit room where shadows were moving and words were being spoken in Russian, a language Mulder recognized but could not understand. Still, he got a certain drift at once: One of those shadowy figures behind the plastic was issuing orders, and the others were responding with crisp acknowledgments of same.

That much Mulder got.

And when he noticed the larger cage, a wooden box with air holes drilled, its door yawning open to reveal a crumpled blanket on the plank floor of what was obviously a cage not for canines but for a human, Mulder knew at once that whatever was going on beyond that curtain needed to be stopped.

Bloodied, dirtied, down to his black T-shirt and jeans, the former agent pushed through the curtain, tire iron poised to do damage.

He barely had time to take in the bizarre operating room when he said, voice cracking but forceful nonetheless, *"Stop what you're doing! And back away *from there . . ."*

The tire iron was raised in a bloody hand as Mulder stepped forward to better make his point. Before him were a tall, older apparent doctor—in a medical gown, cap, and surgical mask—and two nurses or assistants, a man and woman, also in surgical masks, over which wide, startled eyes appraised Mulder.

The medical trio backed up as Mulder approached, the tall old doctor shouting at him in Russian.

Mulder snapped, "Shut up!"

But the doctor kept talking, kept shouting, filling the air with unfathomable Russian as a horrified Mulder finally saw the two patients this "healer" was attending.

On an operating table rested a disembodied head, a male head, the head in fact of Franz Tom-czeszyn, whose donor transplant business had been taken to its ghastly if logical extreme, plastic tubes connecting the man's head to the throat of a nude woman who floated unconscious or nearly so in a big plastic tub of slushy discolored water, blood pumping through those tubes as the missing (and now found) Cheryl Cunningham kept the dis-embodied head of Franz Tomczeszyn alive.

And still the doctor screamed in Russian.

"*Shut up!*" Mulder demanded, and shook the tire iron. "Goddammit, I said shut up! Do you speak English?" He looked to the two assistants. "Do *any* of you speak English?"

The doctor had taken it down a notch but was still spouting angry Russian, while the pair of assistants just stared blankly at Mulder.

"Listen," Mulder said despite their nonresponse. "I want her *out* of there . . . I want those tubes out of her and her neck sewn up. Properly. *Now.*"

But neither assistant seemed to understand, and the tall doctor was still bleating in Russian, adding to this waking nightmare, leaving the weak, hurting Mulder with no idea what to do next . . .

The doctor, however, suddenly stopped speaking and began moving toward the two patients linked by blood-pumping plastic tubes. *Did the old man understand English after all?*

Mulder raised the tire iron, moving closer. "Are you going to do what I said?"

The two assistants backed off, seeking the periphery of the brightly lit operating room, just as the doctor again began to speak in Russian, not yelling now, rather affecting a reasonable tone, gesturing to his two patients as he did.

Mulder said, "I don't understand. I can't *understand* you . . ."

But Mulder was trying to, trying to focus in this hellish situation, and did not see a shadow behind him, a figure in white behind the wall of plastic, from which arms shot through and looped around Mulder's neck, choking him, clutching him.

Mulder twisted, and fought, recognizing Janke Dacyshyn, but not able to squirm loose from the Russian's grasp, and Mulder could not see the tall, gaunt doctor go to a surgical tool tray, make a selection, and turn back with a hypodermic needle, which he jabbed into Mulder's shoulder.

He felt the fight draining out of him, but the darkness came so quick, he didn't notice.

Rural Virginia
January 12

Assistant FBI Director Walter Skinner was at the wheel of the Expedition, driving through the backwoods boonies where the only saving grace was that the snow had stopped. In the rider's seat, Dana Scully stared pensively out at white wilderness gliding by.

Though clenched with concern, Skinner did his best to soothe her: "We're going to find him."

Her nod was barely perceptible.

"I know Mulder," Skinner went on, "and he'd get to a phone first and call. He wouldn't go off and do anything crazy."

Now she looked at him as if to say, *Are you kidding?*

Skinner swallowed. Shrugged. "Not overly crazy."

Scully returned her eyes to the window. He kept glancing at her, and saw her sit up straight. They were passing an unmaintained road, and neither Skinner nor Scully was aware that this lane was one that a plow truck had recently gone down, only to be followed by Fox Mulder on foot. No evidence of that was present for the assistant director and former agent to note, as new snowfall covered both the recent plowing and any tracks.

Skinner wasn't sure what had caught Scully's attention. The moment seemed to have passed and

Scully was settling back in her seat again. They drove for a few seconds in silence, then she turned sharply to Skinner and said, "Stop, please—stop *here . . .*"

He stopped. "What is it, Dana?"

But she was already getting out of the Expedition. When he climbed out and came around, he found her standing surveying a row of twenty rural mailboxes.

"What is it?" he repeated.

She moved down the row, apparently looking for a specific mailbox. *A name, perhaps?* Skinner wondered.

She stopped at one that had an address that had lost a number, leaving it: 25 2.

She was staring at the mailbox.

"Dana?"

"Proverbs."

"What?"

"Proverbs. 25:2." She was shaking her head, her expression stunned but somehow hopeful. "I don't *believe* this . . ."

She yanked open the little door and began pulling out envelopes, junk mail mostly. Skinner had no idea what the hell she was up to, but she was up to *something . . .*

" 'God's glory to hide a thing,' " she was saying. " 'The honor of kings to search it out.' . . . I've *got* it!"

Skinner looked over Scully's shoulder at a letter with a typed address.

"Invoice for medical supplies," she said. "Addressed to a Dr. Uroff-Koltoff. It's *got* to be him."

"Who?"

"The doctor who did the Russian transplants I told you about. He's got an address on Nine Mile Road."

Reflexively, both Skinner and Scully began looking around, up and down the country road. Were any of these lanes marked?

Her eyes were tight, her breath pluming in the cold. "Where the hell is Nine Mile Road!"

Skinner got out his iPhone. "Maybe I can Google it."

"Right. You can type in *mad doctor*." Then she frowned and turned away from him. "You *hear* that? Listen . . . *listen* . . ."

The running engine of the Expedition nearby was a distraction, and she stepped away from it, listening intently. Skinner followed.

"What?" he asked.

"Dogs," she said.

He heard it, too, distant but distinct: barking dogs.

But why, Skinner wondered, did the sound of yipping and yapping light up Dana Scully's face with hope?

The Compound
Rural Virginia
January 12

Fox Mulder could not hear the barking dogs; he lay drugged and unconscious on the floor of the operating room, while the gaunt doctor was issuing orders in Russian to his assistants, loud enough to rise over the dogs but no longer with the edge of anger displayed to their intruder.

That intruder was no longer of concern to any of them, and the doctor and the assistants would even step over him as they continued their freakish work. They barely noticed when Janke Dacyshyn grabbed Mulder under the arms and dragged him out from under their feet, back into the kennel.

Moments later, the Russian banged open a trailer door, stepped out into the cold though he wore only the surgical whites, then reached in and dragged Mulder out of the mobile home onto the muddy pathway. Much as he had dragged many a garbage bag of dismembered limbs for disposal, the Russian now hauled the limp, heavy Mulder out into the fenced-off yard, the cargo's feet making lines in the fresh snow.

About midway on the journey from the conjoined trailers to a small wooden shed in a corner of the compound, Mulder came slowly awake. He had to fight for consciousness, helpless against the drug, not to mention the bruiser who was dragging him toward that ominous shed.

Finally the Russian towed Mulder around to the front of the shed where an axe was propped against a chopping block. A pile of firewood leaned against the side of the shed, but what finally woke Mulder fully was the sight of something else on the muddy ground: *a headless, naked female body.*

And Fox Mulder knew that he had finally found Monica Bannan; she lay facedown—or she would have been, if she'd had a face—near the chopping block and the axe. Moments later Mulder was deposited next to the headless body, and the former agent felt as helpless as Monica Bannan, watching the Russian stop to catch his breath.

Then the Russian came over and Mulder's gut tightened, but the man was after the headless body, which he yanked over to the chopping block, positioning an arm on it, obviously getting ready to chop the body into pieces.

As the Russian raised the axe to begin his grisly job, his hands blistered from the many times he'd performed such a task, the operation within the mobile home continued, a process about to start that was not unrelated to Janke Dacyshyn's current clean-up project.

Franz Tomczeszyn's disembodied head might have seemed just another body part to discard, if it weren't for one thing: The eyes, on occasion, blinked. He was, in a way at least, still alive, joined to Cheryl Cunningham via those blood-delivering tubes that jutted from the incision in her throat.

That same throat was currently the focus of Dr. Uroff-Koltoff's attention, as he lowered a scalpel to the iodine-painted neckline, preparing to sever one head to replace it with another.

In the yard, near the shed, Janke Dacyshyn was moving quicker than the gaunt doctor. His grim dismemberment routine had been quick and efficient as Mulder forced himself to look on, still fighting to regain and retain consciousness so that perhaps he would not end up like Monica Bannan, so many body parts scattered over the ground around a chopping block.

The Russian put the axe down, leaning it against the block once more. He went to Mulder, who was trying to get his muscles, his limbs, working, before they never worked again, and felt himself being positioned atop the chopping block, apparently to remove the head first. Maybe Mulder could roll off, and flee, but could he escape swings of an axe by the pursuing Russian?

The Russian was just raising the axe over Mulder's neck when a voice nearby said, "Hey . . ."

Then Mulder saw something that had to be a drug-induced hallucination: *Scully slamming a piece of chopped wood into the Russian's head, the man's legs buckling as he went down in an unconscious heap among the body parts he'd created.*

Was Mulder dying and imagining this, as his brain was denied oxygen?

Or was Scully really there, holding his head in her hands, saying, "Mulder . . . Mulder . . ."

Inside, in the operating room, Dr. Uroff-Koltoff was carefully cutting the skin on Cheryl Cunningham's neck, in a clean, skilled circle, when the dogs began another spirited round of barking. The doctor hesitated, looking up, and saw a big bald man burst through the plastic curtain to point a pistol at him and give him a hood-eyed look of utter disgust.

"Hands where I can see them," Skinner said, "*now!*"

The two assistants did not speak English, and Dr. Uroff-Koltoff might or might not have, but all three understood the gun in Skinner's hand, and they backed away from the gurneys.

Dr. Uroff-Koltoff was saying something in Russian, in a be-reasonable tone, but Skinner was paying him scant attention, the assistant director's eyes wide now as he took in a sight he would not soon forget: a disembodied head connected by blood-pumping tubes to a naked woman in a slushy tub, whose life had just been spared.

"Lord God," Skinner said.

Scully parted the plastic curtain, and all her years as a doctor, all her time on the X-Files, did not prepare her for this grotesque tableau. But she pushed past the horror, and moving to the gurneys, said to Skinner, "Mulder needs warm clothes and fluids. I want you to do it. I've got work here."

Skinner cuffed Dr. Uroff-Koltoff to a machine and left the two assistants to assist Scully, who was already scrubbing up with typical calm and nervy haste.

Soon Skinner was banging out a trailer door and running across the compound to the woodshed. He quickly checked the very unconscious Russian, cuffed his hands behind him, then went to Mulder, semiconscious on the ground near the woodshed among scattered body parts that had once been a female FBI agent.

"Mulder," Skinner said, kneeling.

Skinner was getting his topcoat off, and Mulder looked up at him through a druggy haze. "Girl . . . inside . . . she needs help . . ."

"Scully's with her," Skinner said, getting the coat around Mulder's shoulders. "The patient's in good hands."

Mulder was staring at Skinner, trying to make sure his eyes were working, that he wasn't hallucinating. "Skinner?"

The assistant director smiled. "I'm glad to see you alive."

"You . . . big . . . bald . . . beautiful man . . . I'm cold."

And Walter Skinner, ignoring the wind, held Mulder close.

Chapter 16 _____

The newspaper headline reminded Fox Mulder of the kind of outré banner you normally saw in supermarket tabloids, but this one happened to appear in a major Washington, D.C., newspaper over an Associated Press story.

FBI ARREST MODERN-DAY DR. FRANKENSTEIN, it said, and the photo that went with it was particularly satisfying to Mulder—Agent Drummy, who'd been called out by Assistant Director Skinner to the compound with other agents working the Monica Bannan disappearance, stood next to a dog cage that had just been loaded into a four-by-four truck, and sitting in that cage, his temporary quarters for transport, was Dr. Uroff-Koltoff, his gaunt features staring out glumly through the wire mesh.

Mulder, sitting in sweater and jeans at his desk in his home office, was back to clipping newspaper stories of strange events—this one just happened to be a strange event in which he'd been caught up. The events of just twenty-four hours before seemed distant now, with only the scuffs and bruises on his face proof that anything unusual had really happened.

"Mulder . . ."

He turned and saw the woman he loved framed in the doorway, a gentle vision in a brown sweater and skirt.

"What's up, Doc?" he asked, playful but careful—they'd been through so much in recent days.

She stepped inside his cluttered, obsessive space, arms folded to herself as if still cold, though the house was toasty. "Father Joe," she said quietly, "is dead."

He sat there stunned for a moment, until she nodded to underscore the truth of her words and said, "He was clearly a very sick man."

Mulder had dropped his scissors but the story about "Dr. Frankenstein" was almost clipped, and he tore it out the rest of the way.

"Did you read this?" he asked, rising, brandishing the clipping. "The FBI's official statement claims disgraced priest Joseph Crissman was an *accom-*

plice in all this . . . not a word about consulting on the case, nothing about his psychic connection."

Her eyebrows went up. "He's dead, Mulder. Gone. He may well have been an accomplice. We'll never really know the truth."

"*I* know, Scully," he said, coming over to her. "And so do you."

"But I don't."

"Oh? Well, I can prove it—he died of bone-marrow cancer, right? Same as the man who Dr. Frankenstein was giving a new body."

"Mulder . . ."

"And what time did you pull the tubes from Cheryl Cunningham's neck? What time did you cut off the blood supply to Franz Tomczeszyn's head?"

Her head tilted, her wary expression telling him she knew exactly where he was headed.

"Because *that's* when Father Joe died, Scully. Get me the death certificate and I'll show you—then I'm going to take it and shove . . . *show* it to the FBI."

Her smile was too sad, too weary, to really be a smile at all. "You really think they'll take your call? Oh, Skinner would—but he'd be overruled, wouldn't he?"

Mulder began to say something, then realized there wasn't really a valid response—Scully was very likely right.

She touched his sleeve. "Let it go, Mulder."

He shook his head. "It's an injustice to the man's name. *Father Joe* saved that woman. We both know it."

This time just one eyebrow went up. "What reputation did he *have* to save? Considering his crimes against those young boys, who's really going to care?"

"I care. And I think you care, too."

She frowned.

"Scully, Father Joe is why Cheryl Cunningham is alive."

"Mulder—*you're* the reason that woman is alive." She shrugged. "And I guess I am, too. And Skinner—no matter what you believe about Father Joe, *that* was the rescue team."

He studied her Madonna's face; she was hiding things behind it. "You said you believed him, too."

She sighed, then carefully said, "I *wanted* to believe. And, yes, you're right, I *did* believe him. And I acted on that belief."

They had started this particular discussion a couple of times over the last twenty-four hours, and this was where it had always broken down.

But he tried anyway: "Why won't you just tell me what Father Joe said to you?"

Scully sighed again. Rolled her eyes. Then, finally if grudgingly, she said, "He told me . . . don't give up."

Mulder didn't know what to say. He understood

at once that the ex-priest's words had not just been about the Monica Bannan case, but also another case, Scully's case, the Fearon boy.

And he knew precisely the dilemma she faced.

"And I didn't give up, Mulder, and it saved your life." She swallowed. "But I put that child through hell, and I've got another surgery scheduled this morning, after I did some very fast talking with his parents . . . and do you know why? Because I believed God was telling me to."

Mulder said nothing; he could see how this was weighing on her.

She said, "I believed God was talking to me, Mulder, through a pedophile priest, no less—a man who violated God's most sacred trust."

And she rolled her eyes again, shaking her head, as if she couldn't believe her own gullibility.

"But *doesn't* it make sense, Scully?" He put a hand on her shoulder. "If Father Joe was seeking redemption, how better than to help save Christian's life? What if Father Joe *was* forgiven? What if his prayers were answered, after all?"

Scully looked up, momentarily putting aside her irritation with herself, and letting Mulder's passion touch her. "Why would they have been? So many prayers go unanswered . . . Why would God choose a sinner like Father Joe?"

He shrugged. "Maybe because . . . he didn't give up . . . ?"

"Riiiight," she breathed. The doubting half smirk was one Mulder had seen many times. "Try and prove *that* one, Mulder."

Even after all he'd seen over the years, Mulder remained unconvinced he could, that anyone could. She was right.

"Anyway," she sighed, "I'm due at the hospital."

Soon, in her coat and boots, valise in hand, Scully was heading out under a sunnier sky into every bit as much snow to their rented sedan, as Mulder in just sweater and jeans watched from the stoop.

"Scully!" he called.

About to get in the car, she turned toward him.

"Why would he say it?" Mulder stepped down from the stoop and walked over to her, breath steaming in the chill. "'Don't give up'? Why would Father Joe say such a thing to you, Scully, who showed him such contempt?"

"It was clearly about you, Mulder. About hanging in and saving that woman."

"But he didn't say it to *me*, and he had plenty of opportunities. It was to you. Why to you, Scully?"

She shook her head, shrugged. "Really, I have no idea."

He gave her a sly smile. "If Father Joe were the devil, why say the opposite of what the devil would say? The devil would send you down a blind alley, not to where some poor woman could be rescued."

That seemed to give her pause. This she hadn't considered . . .

Mulder pressed on: "Maybe *that's* the answer—what God wants. And not just about me or even about the boy or even you, Scully. But all of us."

"What . . . what do you mean?"

"Don't give up."

That seemed to hit her hard, hearing Father Joe's words coming from Mulder; but he could see, as he'd seen so many times, her rational mind kick in and bat back the emotions.

"Please, Mulder," she said, hardly able to look at him. "This is hard enough."

"I know."

He put his arms around her. Held her.

"If you have any doubt, Scully," he whispered, "don't do it. Call off the surgery this morning."

She looked up at Mulder, her face revealing the agony she was working through, to make that decision. But she wasn't avoiding his gaze; she was looking right at him, with love and trust and even hope.

"But either way," he said, brushing hair from her face, "let's get out of here."

She squinted at him, like she hadn't heard right. "Where?"

"Imagine an island with lots of white beach. Imagine lots of blue ocean. You in a swimsuit, and . . ."

"You in a red Speedo?"

"I may still have that somewhere. Just us in a little boat with all that blue and all that sand and we're brown as berries 'cause we're out of the cold and dark and into the warm and light. As far away from the darkness as you and I can get."

She was smiling but it was tinged with sadness. "I don't think you can get away from the darkness, Mulder. I think it finds you."

"I think you're right," he said. Then he smiled. "But let it try."

And he kissed her.

She nodded bravely, touched his face, then he let go of her and watched as she got in the car and drove off.

Don't give up, he thought. *Don't give up.*

Our Lady of Sorrows Hospital
Richmond, Virginia
January 13

Dana Scully, in lab coat and scrubs, studied the medical chart intently as she moved down the corridor. When she glanced up, she saw Father Ybarra at the far end, talking to Christian's parents. She could only imagine that the administrator was making an eleventh-hour effort to talk the Fearons out of going along with her plan of action, after she had worked so long and hard to convince them.

Father Ybarra was not regarding her with a benign expression. Nor, for that matter, were the Fearons. They seemed to expect her to stop and talk, but the time for stopping and talking was past, and Scully, not slowing, said only, "Mr. and Mrs. Fearon. Father . . ."

The priest and the parents nodded, but if any of them had second thoughts, none was expressed as she blew by.

Scully, at the doorway to the operating room, paused and said back to them, pleasantly, "Excuse me," and went in.

The OR was buzzing with activity, nurses readying the room—and young Christian—for surgery. Again the boy's shaved head was affixed within the harsh-looking traction device.

The boy's eyes found Scully's as she entered, and momentarily she was stopped in her tracks. She watched as the anesthesiologist began to ready the child, then she turned to the scrub sink. Once again, fear took hold, as before when Christian faced the first of these procedures; more would be at stake, as the risk grew higher.

She could not meet the eyes of her OR team, who were now set and waiting. Snapping on the latex gloves, she moved to the operating table and again met Christian's gaze.

The boy in the ghastly traction device could not have looked more frail or vulnerable or, for that matter, innocent. His eyes, however, held hers with unblinking maturity, meeting her gaze fearlessly.

Staring down at the boy, frozen, transfixed, she did not sense the OR team exchanging subtle, nervous glances.

Polite if tentative, a nurse asked, "Are you ready to begin, Dr. Scully?"

A voice in her mind said: *Don't give up.*

Not Father Joe, however—Mulder. *Mulder's voice.*

An image flashed through her mind of the couple tanned in a little boat lazily gliding on blue water under a sunny sky near a white beach. She almost smiled.

Then Dana Scully met the boy's gaze with a fearlessness equal to his own.

"Yes," she said to her team. "Let's begin."

The Truth Is in Here

I would like to thank Frank Spotnitz for taking time during the production of *The X-Files: I Want to Believe* to field questions and provide extensive materials. He was unfailingly prompt, friendly, and supportive. In addition to dealing with my queries on an almost daily basis, Frank provided wardrobe breakdowns, location information, and a cast list, all extremely helpful, since I was writing the novel at the same time the film was being shot.

Key among those Frank put me in touch with was Academy Award–winning film editor Richard Harris, who despite his duties on the ongoing production spent several hours on the phone, guiding me through a crucial sequence with skill, patience, and humor.

I would also like to thank Debbie Olshan of 20th

Century Fox and Sarah Durand of HarperCollins for entrusting this novel to me. Also my agent, Dominick Abel; and my wife, Barbara Collins, for her editorial assistance.

Finally, thanks to series creator Chris Carter and (again) Frank Spotnitz, coauthors of the screenplay, for allowing me to be a part of *X-Files*, long after this fan thought such an opportunity would present itself.

Max Allan Collins

MAX ALLAN COLLINS was hailed in 2004 by *Publishers Weekly* as "a new breed of writer." A frequent Mystery Writers of America "Edgar" nominee, he has earned an unprecedented fourteen Private Eye Writers of America "Shamus" nominations for his historical thrillers, winning for *True Detective* and *Stolen Away*.

His graphic novel *Road to Perdition* is the basis of the Academy Award–winning film starring Tom Hanks and directed by Sam Mendes. His comics credits include the syndicated strip *Dick Tracy*; his own *Ms. Tree*; *Batman*; and *CSI: Crime Scene Investigation*, for which he has also written video games and a *USA Today*–best-selling series of novels.

An independent filmmaker in the Midwest, he

has written and directed such features as the Lifetime movie *Mommy* and the recent DVD release *Eliot Ness: An Untouchable Life*. His produced screenplays include the HBO World Premiere *The Expert* and the current *The Last Lullaby*, based on his acclaimed novel *The Last Quarry*.

His other credits include film criticism, short fiction, songwriting, trading-card sets, and movie/TV tie-in novels, among them the national bestsellers *Saving Private Ryan*, *Air Force One*, and *American Gangster*.

Collins lives in Muscatine, Iowa, with his wife, writer Barbara Collins.